RUM AND COKE

Rum and Coke

Three Short Stories from a Furry Convention

⋆

Madison Scott-Clary

ISBN: 978-1-948743-11-2

Rum and Coke

First Edition, 2019.
10 9 8 7 6 5 4 3 2

1 What I Expected 1

2 How Many? 37

3 Again 69

Content Warning: These stories contain descriptions of sex and sexuality. *How Many* contains explicit description of mental health issues. *Again* contains drug use.

What I Expected

Painting their nails had always calmed Sascha down. The simple act of dragging a brush slowly and carefully, following along the contours of the curved nails in smooth strokes, moving deliberately so as not to bump those nails already painted. The whole act seemed to be almost a meditation, calming to the core.

At least, usually it did. It was difficult to contain the nervousness and excitement that filled them, and they found themself anxiously cycling over the list of things that needed doing before they headed out. Clothes: packed. Cat: fed. Tail and paws: in the bag. Phone charger...

Phone charger!

Cursing quietly under their breath, Sascha quickly finished up the last two nails on their right hand—always the hardest—and ran down the hall to snag the charger from the plug by the bed, being mindful of their still-wet nails. No sense in having to clean polish off the wall.

No such luck with the charger, unfortunately, which received a dash of glossy paint.

"And of course. Piece of shit."

Moving slower now, Sascha made their way back to the kitchen table and settled into their chair. They took a few deep breaths to calm themself before delicately twisting the cap off the polish again, straightening up, and working on adding an additional coat to cover up the ding in the polish they'd received from the charger.

"Getting all gussied up for the con?" their housemate asked sleepily, drifting through the kitchen toward the coffee pot. Mike had a way of moving that looked almost effortless, a testament to his laid back life as professional dreamer. Sascha had always admired him for that, along with so many other things.

"Yeah, I figure if there's any one place where I can be assured to not be the weirdest one around, a furry con is probably it."

"Oh, come on," Mike said, rolling his eyes and polishing off the coffee pot to fill his mug. "You're hardly weird around here. College towns are full of people weirder than you, no need to drag yourself through the mud."

Sascha sighed. It was a conversation the two had had enough times before that they didn't feel the need to list out all the counter-arguments they kept in stock. No amount of discussion could seem to dispel the deeper insecurities involved, anyway, much as Mike might try.

So the two shared an easy silence—or perhaps it was easy on Mike's end; Sascha simply held still, fingers splayed, and watched the floor as they waited for the polish to dry. Their mind rolled through waves of anxiety and forced relaxation, focusing on holding still and not simply jittering right out of their chair.

"So," Mike finally said, voice softer than before. "What's got you so nervous? Meeting up with whats-his-face?"

Sascha slumped, "That obvious, huh?" They bought themself a

moment to think by blowing across the nails of one hand, then the other.

"Yeah, meeting Shadow," they continued. "I'm not...really sure what to do. I mean, I really like him, and I guess a con's a safe enough place to meet up with someone, since if it doesn't work out, it's not like you're trapped alone with them with nothing to do but feel awkward. And at least with this one, I can drive home if I absolutely need to."

Mike eased into the chair across from Sascha and nodded, clearing a space for his coffee. "Do you think you'll hit it off, though?"

"Maybe? I mean, we certainly get along well enough online, but you never really know in person until you meet. We talked through that, too, about how maybe things won't line up that well, and how this is just sort of an experiment."

Sascha found it hard to meet Mike's sleepy gaze. They had tried dating each other once, earlier in college before they'd moved in together, and it only took a month or two before the realized how much better friends they made than a couple. They clicked well, just not on a relationship level. Ever since, though, Sascha had a hard time discussing relationship things with Mike. The fact that they now shared an apartment had instilled in them a hesitancy around relationships that had kept them out of anything more serious than a crush or fooling around online. This was the closest Sascha had gotten to another relationship since Mike, and it felt a little exciting, as well as more than a little scary.

"You'll do fine, kiddo," Mike laughed, sipping at his coffee.

The pet name got a smile out of Sascha—the height difference between them and Mike when they were dating had led to them being confused as parent and teenaged child more than once. "I know,

I know. Thanks. And thanks again for watching the cat so I can go be a ridiculous furry."

"Oh, that shithead and I will get along fine. We'll totally ignore each other except around dinner time."

"Sounds about right, yeah."

Mike finished his coffee and stood again, wafting easily toward the hall and giving Sascha's shoulder a squeeze on the way out. "Good luck, kiddo, for real. Call me if you need."

⋆

Sascha managed to make it through the rest of the morning without dinging any more nails, a real accomplishment. They had already packed up clothes and furry gear, and got the over-stuffed backpack into the back of their shitty Civic. They even managed to only turn around and retrieve a forgotten item once (the phone charger, natch), and that before they hit the highway. The trip was off to a good start, all told.

The drive itself was uneventful, a mere two hours from home down to the hotel hosting the convention. They were pretty confident that some of their friends would already be there, and thus would provide some distraction from the way their stomach seemed to be doing its level best to pirouette inside their abdomen.

Sascha had moved comfortably through the furry fandom for more than a decade now, having found it sometime in high-school, sticking with it through college, and into post-college life. More so than any other community, furry had helped them through some of the toughest parts of their life, from the divorce of their parents, to coming out—first as gay, then genderqueer—to moving away from home life. They'd tried to fit themself into countless other structures: gender and sexuality support groups, writing groups in college, all with more or less the same result: fading interest, spotty attendance, and eventually moving on.

The most comfortable thing about the fandom was that it provided a place for them to be themself. At times, pretending to be an animal person on the internet was almost ancillary to the sense of community, of just being able to feel comfortable with friends, something they'd never experienced in more structured environments such as all those carefully curated groups and meetups.

And furry is where they had met Shadow.

Shadow was, as his name suggested, a black wolf. Wolves were one of the more common species out there in the furry community, and Sascha had even known a different wolf named Shadow years back. Despite the rather plain name and everyday species, Sascha had found him to be a sweet, mature person who had seemed genuinely interested in them.

They had made an unusual, even rather awkward couple, Shadow the wolf and Sascha—or Skylark, online—the mink. Sascha had initially resisted getting much closer than friendship with Shadow, but he had eventually won them over. They had spent countless hours talking, role-playing everything from going for walks together to sexual encounters, and otherwise getting to know each other over the last four or five months. They'd even had a few short, tense phone calls, something Sascha avoided at all costs, getting to know each others' voices.

Shadow had seemed open to Sascha's gender identity and expression, saying that while he generally considered himself more straight than anything, he was willing to explore outside his normal comfort zone. They had both agreed that sex may not even be a thing for them, as it tended to make Sascha uncomfortable and Shadow had said he wasn't exactly sure what all he would enjoy with someone of indeterminate gender who nonetheless lacked a vagina. It was that open-mindedness that had convinced Sascha that meeting up, even if it wound up only being casual, would be okay.

Now, making their way down the highway and trying to drown out the rattling dash with music, Sascha felt less sure than ever that this was a good idea. Mike and their other friends had been pushing for them to find more of a relationship for years now. They knew their friends were right, too, given how much they talked about companionship and how much that meant to them. Still, though, this just felt like all the scenarios their parents had warned them about, and here they were deliberately going into it.

They shook their head and settled back into the seat. They were committed to going. They'd been telling themself that for weeks, now, and now that they were more than halfway to the hotel, where they'd already reserved a room. There was definitely no turning back.

⋆

"Well if it isn't Skylark, pretty as always."

The voice from behind the chair Sascha had managed to commandeer in the lobby made them jump, startled at first, then hit with recognition. "Maverick! Holy hell, I didn't know you were planning on making it down this weekend!"

They jumped up out of the seat, tail smacking against the coffee table nearby. They remembered to put their purse on the chair to claim it as best as possible, and dashed around to throw their arms around Maverick, who picked them up in a tight squeeze in turn.

"I managed to wrangle some time off. I'm only down here through Sunday at stupid-o'clock in the morning, but hey, at least I made it."

Sascha settled down once Maverick let them go and straightened their skirt out, nodding. "Well, still, glad you could. It's been forever since I've seen you. Haven't caught up with any of the rest of the crew, I figure I'm probably here a little earlier than most."

"Oh, well, I'm here, and I know Volare's around somewhere, I ran into him at the bar, naturally."

"Of course, I'd expect nothing less."

Maverick laughed, straightening his badges and lifting Sascha's purse from the chair before plopping down into it, "I'm sure the bar's gonna make plenty good money this weekend."

Sascha snagged their bag from their friend. Online, Maverick was a rather glowy cheetah whom they'd known for years, and met several times in person at local meets. They settled for sitting down on the arm of the overstuffed chair, leaning against Maverick and draping their stuffed tail across his lap. The two caught up on recent happenings—who was quitting furry forever, what art had caused a big stir among their group of friends, what they had been saving up to buy in the dealer's den this year.

It was Maverick who finally broached the subject of Shadow.

"So when does your...uh...guy friend get here? You've been looking left and right since I spotted you."

"Not until later tonight," Sascha sighed. "I'm just so nervous, I can't stop thinking maybe he'll somehow magically get here early."

"Excited, huh?"

"I'm not even sure it's that, really. Just nervous."

Maverick furrowed his brow. “What, do you think it won’t go well or something?”

Sascha buried their face in their hands and trailed their fingers up through their hair, freshly dyed a subdued red just for the occasion, mumbling behind their forearms, “Yes. Well, no. I mean...I guess I don’t really know. I haven’t been this close to someone since Mike, so it just feels so weird. I don’t know what to do about it.”

Maverick nodded and brought a hand up to rub up over Sascha’s back, tracing along their spine soothingly. “You’ll do fine, minkypie, and you know you’ve got a bunch of us here to take care of you if things don’t go well. They will, though, trust me. Shadow’s a little plain, given the rest of us, but he’s good people.”

“Oh, come on, he’s not that plain. You just say that because your spots glow blue and Volare’s bright pink. By your standards, I’m plain.”

“That you are, girlie.”

Sascha groaned and draped herself dramatically across Maverick’s lap, “Girlie, huh? I haven’t been called that since...well, ever. Congrats on being the first.”

“Skylark the delicate minkygirl, plain as day, swooning wildly into the muscle-bound arms of her manly wolf lover.”

Sascha’s groan turned into giggles, muffled by their hands as they hid their face. “Seriously? I should hit you for that. And lay off the ‘girlie’ and ‘her’ nonsense.”

“Oh? Feeling more boyish of late?” Maverick asked, still grinning.

Sascha sat back up on the arm of the chair, twisting around to settle more comfortably against their friend as they toyed with the fluff at the tip of their tail, “A little, I guess. Maybe it’s the possibility of meeting up with Shadow, though. I don't want to come across as...as...I don't know, disingenuous."

"Hey now, I've heard you talk about gender enough to know that you're hardly disingenuous about it. You talk convincingly enough to get me doubting my own gender, for Christ's sake. Shadow really has you feeling more like a boy?"

"Um, there's just...it's just...there's more to it than that, I guess. I've been honest with him and all, but he's so much more, well, active than I am. I don't want to surprise him or anything."

"Because you interact with him mostly as a girl online?"

"Yeah and..." Sascha stammered for a bit, hunting for the best way to convey the way they'd been feeling. "And I just don't want him to think I'm dishonest or anything."

"Hey mink," Maverick said soothingly, "I don't think you're being dishonest, and I don't think Shadow will think you're being dishonest, either. If you've talked about gender already, then I don't think there's anything you need to worry about. Heck, you're wearing a skirt and have your hair done up all nicely, you're certainly not looking boyish."

Sascha couldn't think of much to add, nodding and murmuring a quiet "thanks" in reply.

The two sat for a little longer, watching the congoers and confused non-attendees streaming past the lobby chairs in various amounts of costume.

It was Maverick's phone buzzing that brought their attention back to the moment.

"Oh, hey, Volare found Vish, and they're at the bar, want to go meet up with them?"

Sascha gave one last look around searching for the buzz-cut that they knew they would spot first, that first sign of Shadow, then finally nodded, "Sure, I could use a drink, anyway."

⋆

The initial meeting between Skylark and Shadow was widely panned by critics as a romance, though some praised its comedic aspects.

By nine that night, Sascha was still in the bar, nursing their second Manhattan and making sure that Volare stayed on his stool more often than not. Maverick had gone off to the restroom something like fifteen minutes ago, and Vish, a non-drinker, was looking more than a little hemmed in. Everything was that delightfully confused mix-up of a convention, and everyone was settling into it in their own way.

"Your hair is...redder than I was expecting."

Sascha whirled. The voice was undoubtedly Shadow's—Peter's—recognizable from the phone. And sure enough, the buzz-cut towering nearly a foot over their own head had them immediately feeling dwarfed. The second thing to catch Sascha's attention was the crash and tinkle of not one, but two glasses as the back of their stool knocked into the bar table and tipped both Volare's and Vish's drinks.

Rather than rushing to hug their partner as they had immagined, Sascha was overcome by an intense feeling of self-consciousness and guilt at what they'd done. They quickly helped pick up pieces of glass and ice, mopping up spilled beer and soda while muttering hasty apologies to their friends. In the process, they managed to cut open a finger on a piece of glass, adding to the confusion.

"Whoa, whoa! Slow down. Skylark!"

By the time Peter had gained their attention, Sascha was fighting to hold back tears and refusing to meet anyone's gaze, never mind that of their boyfriend.

The waitress rushed over to the table with a rag and a bandage for Sascha, and was helping to clean up the sticky mess. She commented on how lucky everyone was to have been spared the deluge for the most part—Volare and Vish both had only a few scattered droplets on their shirts, the rest of the beer-soda flood having made its way onto the floor.

Sascha managed to pry their eyes from the mess and look sheepishly up to Peter, who simply held his arms out. No leaping to the offer of a hug, nor collapsing, weeping, into his arms. Instead, they hesitated for a few seconds—long enough for the entire table to go silent—before slowly leaning into the offered embrace, covering their face with their hands and crying as quietly as possible as Peter held them.

"I'm sorry, that was...that didn't go as planned," Sascha said, once they were sure their voice wouldn't crack.

"Hey, hey. It's okay. I'll just take it as you were really happy to see me. Everything's okay."

"Sorry, I'm just a little anxious, awkward..."

Peter leaned down and placed a tentative kiss to the top of Sascha's head, cooing gently, "It's okay, I promise. Come on, let's sit back down, and we can grab a drink and relax and catch up. You look really good, by the way."

Sascha felt a good portion of their tension melt away at the relaxing murmuring of their partner, enough that they could disentangle their own arms enough to slip around Peter's stocky middle and finally return the hug, taking comfort in the fact that he practically enveloped their smaller frame.

Eventually, Sascha let go and dried their eyes, tugging another stool over for Peter and introducing him to the crowd, most of whom he'd known online for the last few months of hanging out with his partner, and a few of whom he was just meeting for the first time. Peter made his dramatic arrival up to everyone by covering a replacement beer and soda for Volare and Vish, another Manhattan for Sascha, and a beer for himself.

"So," said Volare, sitting up as straight as he could, a sure sign of his drunkenness. "You're the Shadow that we've been hearing so much about! You and Skylark make a really cute couple."

While Sascha hid their face behind their drink, Peter grinned widely and nodded, "It's been an interesting few months for me—for both of us, I think. I don't think Sky was really looking for much in the way of a relationship, and I wasn't really looking for someone like him." Realizing his mistake quickly, he rushed to add, "Er, them. I'm sorry, Sky..."

Sascha hunched their shoulders in an attempt to get even smaller, feeling the attention shift from Peter to themself. "It's...it's okay. I appreciate the correction."

Vish and Volare let their gaze linger on the couple, one smiling and the other looking nervous.

"Anyway," Peter continued, hoarsely. "I think it's worked out well, there should be plenty to do this weekend, anyway."

Feeling their courage return after having tripped over themself so much early on, Sascha nodded. "That's why cons are so awesome. We can all hang out together, and we automatically have stuff to do."

Maverick finally made his way back to the table, having been gone for nearly half-an-hour on some minor adventure. Introductions were made and the conversation began to wind comfortably around the group, settling into rhythms at once familiar from all the time they'd spent together online, and foreign in this strange and new setting. A hotel, Sascha decided, was not the most comfortable of places, but the convention was a sort of force working actively against that, bringing comfort to a comfortless place.

⋆

"Sky, I'm really sorry about earlier, I promise I'll do better about the pronouns thing."

Sascha laughed and leaned themself in against Peter, slipping their hand into his and entwining their fingers. "Oh, don't worry about that. I dumped my friends' drinks all over them and fucked up my finger in the process of trying to say hi to you, I'm pretty sure I'm the one that owes you the apology."

Peter laughed as well, and the two of them settled in to the bed they would be sharing for the rest of the con. They had splurged for this trip since Sascha wouldn't be flying and Peter was paid fairly well. They'd gotten a room to themselves with a king bed, and had piled all the myriad pillows up against the headboard in order to create a sort of cozy nest for themselves. After an evening of drinking and watching Volare get drunker than everyone, they had felt the need for a space that was quiet and soft. It was here that Sascha felt most at ease, opening up around Peter, leaning closer and closer to him as they had talked, getting more and more affectionate.

"Sky, I promise, it's fine! I'm just, uh...I'm just really happy to see you. Like, I don't think I've been this happy to meet someone for the first time in a long time."

Sascha tucked themself comfortably against Peter and nodded bashfully, "It's really good to get the chance to actually meet up in person, and I'm really glad-"

They were cut short as Peter fumblingly nudged their head toward his and pressed a shy kiss to their lips. The kiss lingered for a brief second or two before Peter settled back, averting his gaze and admitting shyly, "I, ah...I just wanted to...have wanted to for a while."

"It's okay," murmured Sascha, twisting a little to face Peter more directly and slipping their arms around him. "I'm not complaining one bit."

Peter smiled and helped to tug Sascha a little closer to him, saying, "I've never really kissed...I mean, I guess I should say I've only really kissed girls...er...women in my life. Oh...that sounded bad..."

Sascha laughed and leaned up to kiss Peter once more, shaking their head. "It's fine, Shadow, really. Is it any different?"

"Ohh, I dunno," he said, trying to pull what was obviously his best attempt at a sly look. "Might have to continue experimenting to find out."

Peter, Sascha discovered, tasted slightly of beer, and slightly of the sea, in some inexplicable way. Mike had never been much for kissing, though it was something Sascha had always found to be enjoyably intimate, so they relished the opportunity. Peter was an active kisser, too, leading his partner through his actions, guiding them with his hands on their sides and back, first closer to his side, then, with a gentle tug, up into his lap, leading Sascha to straddle his thighs and lean against him as he leaned back on the headboard. The kisses grew in intensity, as did the tension in both of their bodies.

"Mmn, slow down, just a sec," Sascha whispered, pulling back.

"Everything alright, mink?" Peter asked, looking concerned.

"Yeah just...just need to slow down for a few, little bit of vertigo, feels a little sudden."

"Okay, didn't mean to rush, that was just really nice."

Sascha smiled and slipped their arms up around Peter's shoulders, "It was nice. Very nice, trust me. Just needed a second." They relaxed against his front and calmed their breathing, "Did you figure out if kissing me was different?"

Peter laughed at the question and nodded, "It is, but damned if I know how. Maybe it's just that everyone kisses different, who knows."

Sascha grinned and nodded, "Thought so. Here, lets just get a little more comfy on the bed and we can go back to exploring."

Through concerted effort, the two slid a little further down onto the bed so that Peter rested mostly on pillows instead of the headboard, and Sascha was able to rest their weight more evenly against his front, stretching almost luxuriously along him as they leaned up to meet him in another kiss, moving more slowly and deliberately this time. Tongues teased at each other and hands gripped at shoulders as the couple worked on gaining the comfort that had come so quickly online in a new context.

This time, as the kisses grew more intimate, Sascha quelled their anxiety and opened themself to Peter's obvious desire. They clutched themself closer to him with hands on his shoulders and pressed warmly to his front, feeling the way he moved slightly against them, feeling the slight bulge of his erection grow into a firm ridge against their thigh, feeling his hands move down to the small of their back and pull them to him as his hips nudged gently upwards.

"This okay?" he breathed quietly. Sascha nodded in reply and pressed gently down to him in time with his own motions, slipping back into the comfort and intimacy of the kisses. Their mind was focused on that warmth, focused on making sure that Peter felt as good as they could make him in the moment. Their own arousal, much more constrained by panties and an undershaper, felt secondary to sharing the moment.

Over time, Peter's motions became more insistent and he rolled the two of them onto their sides, still clutching close as he ground his hips firmly to Sascha's. Kisses grew more passionate and hands rubbed along sides and back as the couple rocked together in the bed, both seeming content to be simply be that close, even fully clothed.

Sascha's nervousness began to pick up once more at the thought that Peter might want to go further than simple grinding and kissing in bed, unsure if they were ready to feel that exposed before someone they had just met in person for the first time earlier that evening. However, Peter broke the kiss first and gave a sudden buck of his hips, then shuddered in Sascha's arms, letting out a shaky moan that trailed off into something like a sigh.

Understanding dawned on Sascha and a feeling of intense emotional warmth overrode their anxiety. They simply clung tightly to their lover as he shook gently against them, reveling in the feeling of someone experiencing the rush of pleasure in climax so close to them, sharing in that through proximity as best as they could. There was too much fabric in the way to feel much more than a gentle pulsing of that firm ridge pressed to their thigh, but Sascha could tell that the orgasm was intense, if unexpected.

"S-sorry," moaned Peter, turning his head slightly toward the covers as if to hide his face. "I think...I think I was a little more pent up than I thought..."

Sascha, practically purring in contentment, replied quietly, "No, no, it's okay. That was actually really delightful. Are you okay?"

Peter worked to calm his breathing as he slowly settled down against Sascha, nodding. "I'm fine...I'm fine. Though I'll need to change pants before too long. Um...thank you, Sky."

Sascha laughed and pulled themself even closer to Peter, placing a delicate kiss at the corner of his mouth and marveling at how perfect it felt to be so close.

⋆

Sascha woke slowly, curled at the edge of the bed, to the gentle sound of Peter's snoring—quiet enough to be more endearing than annoying. They had fallen asleep in a tangle of limbs, once they'd gotten cleaned up and into pajamas, but, as had always been the case in Sascha's experience, had separated during the night and slept in late on opposite sides of the bed.

The evening of drinking, talking, intimacy, climax, and more quiet talking drifted back into focus, and Sascha curled up a little tighter, smiling against their pillow at the memory. That things had wound up heading in the direction of sex wasn't all that surprising, given how the two generally acted online. Sex had loomed large in their relationship, and although the idea of getting too much further into it still made Sascha nervous, they found themself relaxing in a warm afterglow the next morning. The simple act of being so close to someone during such an intense moment filled them with happiness. Even if they themself hadn't reached climax, it still felt as though they had gotten a chance to share something special.

"Mmmf, morning."

Sascha was startled out of their reverie by Peter's quiet mumbling, smiling, "Hey, morning."

Peter tugged the covers up under his chin seemingly still asleep, but after a minute or two of silence, he asked, "Time is it?"

Sascha yawned and peeked back over their shoulder at the alarm clock, "Nine-ish, bit after."

Peter nodded and rolled onto his back, muttering, "Sleep. Gooood."

With a quiet laugh, Sascha shifted closer to him under the covers until they were nestled in against his side, head resting on his shoulder and arm slipped over his front, finding the most comfortable way to fit against him. Peter slipped his own arm around their shoulders and rumbled quietly in contentment, though he still hadn't managed to open his eyes.

The two stayed like that for half an hour more, Sascha nearly dozing off before Peter finally stretched out and yawned. He tilted his head down to kiss lightly at Sascha's forehead, leaving behind a gentle tingle from the soft, not unpleasant bristle of his stubble.

Sascha leaned up to return the kiss, but after a moment Peter turned his head to the side, then carefully slipped out from under their arm to stand up out of bed.

"Mm? Is everything alright?" Sascha asked.

"Just wasn't expecting...I mean, would it be okay if you shaved?"

Sascha brought their hand up to feel their own unshaven face—

barely a hint of coarseness, but enough to feel—and felt their body tense. They nodded and sat up in bed, crossing their arms over their knees and settling their chin down behind them, doing their best to hide any shadow that might be showing, "I'm sorry."

"It's okay," Peter mumbled, slipping into a T-shirt. "I just wasn't expecting it, I guess."

Sascha nodded again and slid quietly out of bed, grabbing a change of clothes—jeans today—and their toiletries bag and headed for the shower, hoping they'd remembered their razor.

*

The embarrassment didn't last long. A good shower fixes a lot of things, and Sascha always felt better after shaving, often to the point of doing it twice a day to ensure they had as little shadow and stubble as possible. It was one of those things that wouldn't go away without an investment, and they'd had enough trouble scraping up for this splurge of attending the con.

Sascha thought back to the previous day's conversation with Maverick about not wanting to appear dishonest to Peter about gender. They winced, but got themself cleaned up well and even added a touch of makeup, just a bit of concealer and eyeshadow to feminize their features somewhat. Something conciliatory to make things go a little more smoothly. Soon, that warm afterglow they had felt before was back, along with a smile.

Getting dressed, they belted on their tail and opted for fuzzy paws instead of shoes. Now that the con would be in full swing, it wouldn't hurt to furry things up a little. After all, just paws and a tail would put them at the low end of the dress-up spectrum.

Sascha packed up their kit and slunk out of the bathroom to find Peter gathering his own things up for a quick shower. They leaned down and kissed him lightly on the cheek, "This better, Shadow?"

He smiled up to them bashfully and nodded, "Sorry about before. I know it wasn't very nice of me. I just was caught off guard."

"No, it's alright. I don't like it either. Go ahead and get ready, and we can get some food. There's a coffee shop down the street that does good breakfast burritos."

While Peter showered, Sascha caught up on how their friends' nights had been. Volare had gotten drunk, of course. Vish had gotten upset, of course. Maverick had apparently spent much of the evening trawling the lobby and Friday night dance in hopes of running into anyone else he knew with little luck. His job kept him busy enough that he wasn't totally in touch with the furry scene, so it wasn't a big surprise. A few more of Sascha's friends and acquaintances had shown up, and they made a note to say hi at some point during the day.

They spent a few minutes poking at Twitter, drafting message after message

> Fantastic night last night :)

Delete delete.

> Really good evening, so good to meet up with @ShdwWolf.

Delete delete delete.

> Good evening last night. Caught up with friends, had a fantastic time with @ShdwWolf. Glad I could make it.

They pondered for a second before hitting send. It would be enough to state that the night had been positive without necessarily tipping their hand as to how positive it had been for them.

Peter eventually made his way out of the bathroom, clean-shaven and damp, and smiled to Sascha. They finished getting dressed—standard furry wear of con shirts, jeans, paws, and tails—and made their way to the elevators.

Sascha leaned against Peter's arm in the elevator, taking his hand in their own. He smiled down to them and gave a little wagging motion of his backside. It made Sascha laugh.

Once in the lobby, they ran into Maverick looking bored, and roped him into going to grab breakfast and coffee with them. The three chatted amiably as they made their way to the coffee shop and through the line to order, each getting a breakfast burrito or other treat and a coffee drink to finally wake up.

Peter excused himself to go wash his hands, and Maverick pounced. He took Sascha's hands in his own and grinned widely at his friend. "So! A fantastic time, huh?"

Sascha did their best to not look embarrassed, "Yeah, it was a good evening all around."

"Come on, you're glowing!"

"What? Am not!"

"Trust me. Take it from the glowy cheetah. You're glowing."

Sascha couldn't do much other than bow their head to keep their blush from being seen.

"It's good, minky," Maverick continued, voice softening. "I won't pry, I'm just happy for you."

Sascha smiled shyly and drew one of their hands back, enough to take a sip of their coffee and hide their face for a moment. "It was a good and comfortable night. We didn't...you know, do much, but it was just good."

"Well, hey, 'good' is what cons are for. Oh, hey Shadow, promise I'm not mackin' on your mink."

Peter pulled his chair up to the table and grinned, adopting an air of incredulity, "Macking? Really?"

"Yeah, come on, Maverick. We left the nineties behind a while back," Sascha laughed.

Later that day, by the time they'd made it back to the hotel and met up with Volare, an icy Vish, and a few others from the IRC channel they all hung out on, the glow that had obviously suffused Sascha had calmed down to a sense of peace and happiness. They were pleased to tag along after Peter and the crew as they made their way slowly through the dealer's den, ogling books and art, carefully noting commission prices (and snagging one or two that were within their range), and just generally being a giggly group of friends.

⋆

The day wound down slowly, and since all had been out and about on their feet all day, none were all that keen on heading to the dance. Dinner had been a simple, if stressful affair at an overcrowded sandwich place.

Afterwards, everyone had decided to congregate in Maverick, Volare, and Vish's room. The fourth member, Anna, hadn't been able to make it to the con, and they hadn't been able to pick up anyone else by the time the con rolled around, so Maverick had a bed to himself while Volare and Vish alternated between cuddling and arguing in their own bed.

Volare had, of course, procured a fifth of rum and a two-liter bottle of coke, despite Vish's grumbling. Everyone sat down on the beds and the single office chair, passing around one of the two water glasses filled with rum and coke, while Vish claimed the second glass as his own without any rum. Eventually, Peter caved and ran up the one flight of stairs to his and Sascha's room to get a few more glasses.

"So how's it goin', Sky?" Volare asked, his voice perfectly level, but the redness in his cheeks showing that he'd had two rum-and-cokes to everyone else's one. "With Shadow, I mean. Seems like things are going well."

Sascha blushed as Maverick immediately laughed. "Ignore him. Things are going well. We had a good night, and today was good. It feels...I don't know. It just feels good to be close to someone again. Some awkwardness, you know, with the gender thing. Nothing bad, just kinda finding ways to work it out, I guess."

Volare nodded, hugging an arm around Vish next to him. "You sure everything's okay, though? I hate to go all motherly-gay-dude over you, but I just want to make sure."

Passing the last of the drink off to Maverick, Sascha nodded. "I think so. I worry that I'm too outside of the realm of experience, for him, though it seems like he's trying, in his own way."

Volare nodded again, and a silence fell over the room as Maverick set about mixing another drink, this one stronger than the last. He was larger than anyone in the room (though that was hardly a stretch, given how small Volare and Sascha were), and tended to make things to his own tastes and constitution.

There was a quick knock on the door, and Sascha jumped up to open it, letting Peter back in carrying two glasses and a small metal flask. "I've got the glasses, and I've also got some crappy whiskey some rando in the hall filled my flask with. Evan Williams or something equally awful."

"Mmm, shitty bourbon," drawled Volare.

The group laughed and welcomed him back into the circle, letting him take his spot by Sascha. He poured a finger or two of whiskey into one of the glasses and beckoned for the coke, passing the other glass to Maverick in exchange, then topped off his own glass with soda.

The pleasant banter continued around the room, minus the bits about Peter now that he was there. At some point someone put some music on through their cell phone, though later, Sascha was hard pressed to say who exactly had done so. Something chill, calm, something to fill the silences when conversation waned.

Sascha noted that, when he wasn't drinking from the communal rums-and-coke going around the circle, Peter was also sipping from the flask that he carried, and quite obviously getting drunker as the night went by. That was okay, though, they figured. They were drinking plenty, themself, and it was good to feel the warm buzz surrounding everyone as the night wore on. Even Vish seemed to be getting in the spirit, laughing along with jokes and getting closer and closer to Volare through the night.

"'m glad you all seem pretty cool with me tagging along like this. Know I'm new to the channel and all, but I'm glad Sky put in a good word for me," Peter said quietly during one of the little lulls in the talking.

Maverick, always a happy person and a happier drunk, laughed and leaned over to give Peter an awkward sort of sideways hug. "Of course, man, you seem cool, and I know we trust Sky."

Peter returned the half-hug and grinned to himself, looking sleepy. “Yeah, he’s a good mink,” he said, sounding satisfied.

The silence lingered on for a few seconds before Sascha hunched their shoulders and quietly murmured, “ ‘They’re’.”

Peter laughed loudly and hugged his arm around Sascha’s shoulders, pulling them firmly toward his side. Definitely drunk. “He, they, whatever. You can be my good little minkyboy too, right?”

The silence continued to stretch out, glances were exchanged. Eventually Sascha sat up a little straighter, trying to look as dignified as their drunk self could manage. “I’m not feeling very boyish. I know I’m maybe not as much of a girl as you’d like, but I’m not a boy.”

There were a few nervous laughs around the group, but Peter furrowed his brow. “I’m trying to compliment you, Sky. I think you make as good a boy as a...as a...as a whatever.”

Sascha watched Peter fall into a sulk and frowned. They didn’t feel like there was much that they could do. The drunk reasoning with the drunk is a fancy way of talking in circles.

It was Vish, of all people, who saved them the trouble. “Hey, it’s getting late, and I want to crash. Sounds like folks have stuff to work out, too, so maybe we can catch up tomorrow?”

Maverick caught on and stood up right away, only wobbling a little bit. “Hey, Shadow, was really good to get the chance to catch up. I’m out early in the morning, so...” he trailed off, offering Peter a hug, as was customary.

Peter struggled to his feet and leaned silently into Maverick’s hug, then seemingly on impulse, hugged Vish and Volare as well. He straightened up deliberately and made his way back to Sascha, who had made it to their feet by then as well, and held their hand, firmly entwining fingers with fingers.

"Drive safe, Maverick. See you guys later," Sascha offered, trying to sound light-hearted

*

"I feel like I've let you down," Sascha said quietly. "I feel like I've lied to you."

Peter stomped up the stairs, two steps ahead of them. "Tell me about it."

Sascha followed on in silence up the next flight and out the door by the ice machine, making their way after Peter down the hallway to their room. They unlocked the door and entered in silence, Sascha sitting carefully on the bed and Peter falling gracelessly into the desk chair. Silence, thick and tangible, hung between them.

"I feel like we had a really good night last night," Sascha offered, after a minute or two. "I feel like we connected in a really important way-"

Peter cut them off, "I feel like I was imagining you as my little girl, like you were the person I've been imagining the whole time these last six months."

Sascha fell quiet again. They stood, paced to the end of the bed, paced back, sat again, and stood once more. Finally, they buried their face in their hands and mumbled, "I'm sorry. I'm not trying to...you know, be difficult. I want to be that person for you, I just...there's just so only so much I can do."

"You could've not been..." Peter started. "You could've acted like what I should have expected from the start. You're not really what I expected at all."

Sascha clenched their fists and stuffed them into the pockets of their hoodie, "I want to be something good for you, that's all I've ever wanted to be. I don't know how to be anything else."

Peter looked away in silence.

Sascha lowered their head, closed their eyes, and resumed their pacing circuit. They didn't look at Peter, they didn't look at the ground, they simply paced and did their best to cut out all input. Anxiety welled in their chest like some awful, noxious bubble aiming to burst in the form of some horrible meltdown. They focused on breathing. Count of four in, hold for a count of five, count of seven out. Anything to calm the situation, even if only internally.

"Here, I'll tell you what you can do, sweets," Peter slurred, sounding half angry, half something else.

Looking up, Sascha found that Peter had unzipped his fly and tugged his boxers down, and was aiming his erection in their direction. "Even boyminks got warm muzzles, hmm?"

Sascha was shocked. Their head was spinning, and they couldn't tell if it was from the alcohol or the proposition.

"Well, c'mon, you were eager enough last night, though you must've had some rockin' panties on, didn't feel a thing," Peter sneered.

"You want me to give you a blow job," Sascha asked incredulously. "But you just said I wasn't what you expected."

"Come on. Bygones and all that crap. Take care of me and I'll forget about all this gender shit. I came here thinking we'd have a good time together, so let's have a good time."

The combination of vague threats and an act that Sascha had rehearsed in their mind over these past few months countless times—had acted out through role-play online with Peter more than once—

was too much for them to handle. Their mouth went dry, they couldn't swallow, the room seemed closer and closer.

"Fuck it," they whispered. "Fuck you, if you think sex'll clear this mess up."

And they stepped out the door.

⋆

Sascha made it to the stairwell before the tears hit, and when they did hit, they hit silently and with no force, simply spilling down over their cheeks and into the waiting sleeve at the crook of their elbow. Growing up a boy, taught to be a man, had left them much that needed to be unlearned, but the secret of crying quietly when one was supposed to be strong felt like an inheritance of sorts.

Their phone buzzed. Twitter.

> fine
>
> Direct message from @ShdwWolf

The tears came harder.

⋆

> SkylarkMink: you awake?
>
> Mavcheets: Just getting ready. What's up. You okay?
>
> SkylarkMink: no.
>
> SkylarkMink: can i come by
>
> Mavcheets: Sure, just be quiet. V and V are asleep, was packing

⋆

Sky I'm sorry, drank too much :(

Direct message from @ShdwWolf

⋆

Sky, take your time, but please come back :(

Direct message from @ShdwWolf

⋆

Mav sent me a dm, can we talk

Direct message from @ShdwWolf

⋆

Mav says your okay and sleeping there, talk tomorrow pls? :(

Direct message from @ShdwWolf

⋆

Sascha awoke neatly wrapped in Maverick's—they still didn't know his real name—arms when their friend's alarm went off. Maverick was well attuned to his alarm and reached across Sascha to turn it off with ease before returning to the hug that had apparently lasted all night, burying his face against the back of Sascha's neck.

They had fallen asleep with their clothes on, for lack of any pajamas. The night had drawn out for another hour or so of whispered conversation in bed, keeping quiet lest they way Volare and Vish. Sascha had fallen asleep dressed and crying, but safe against their friend, feeling his bulk behind them as something of comfort rather than as a source of anxiety.

Maverick had done admirably. He'd asked if everything was okay several times, and gotten the full story of what had happened after Sascha and Peter had left. He didn't pass any judgements on either of them, and had let Sascha talk until they had started to doze.

Even so, Sascha wasn't sure what to make of the remainder of the evening. Everything felt so safe with Maverick and so...well, cold with Peter. They were hesitant as always to draw conclusions on that—just because a friend was nice to them when something had gone wrong didn't mean that...well, it meant that he was a good friend. To be honest, their first instinct had been to take Mike up on his offer to call whenever, but it had been so late, and only a little bit since they had left Maverick's room in the first place with alcohol buzzing through them. Nothing to feel sorry about.

Except Peter.

Maverick grunted and leaned up on an elbow in bed behind them, then leaned forward to give a friendly kiss to their cheek. "Hey, morning. I gotta start getting ready, but you sleep in, okay? I'll send V and V a note explaining that you needed a place to stay for the night and took my bed."

Sascha curled themself a little tighter in bed and nodded silently.

"You keep in touch, okay hon?" he murmured, giving one last gentle squeeze. "And be safe, minkypie. Things got rough, but you've got friends here."

"Thank you," whispered Sascha, clutching briefly at Maverick's hand before letting him get up and get ready to drive.

⋆

Later that morning, once Volare and Vish had woken up and learned what Sascha would tell them of the night before, they made plans to get them back to their room. The two flanked them as they made their way up the flight of stairs and preceded them into the room in case Peter was still in there and upset.

Instead, they found the room to be empty, and Sascha followed after to find the room neatly kept—the bed made hastily and Peter's clothes stacked neatly atop his bag. The bathroom was humid, a shower taken there not long before.

"At same coffee shop, meet me there?" read a small note on the desk.

"That's good," remarked Volare. "A question you don't have to answer. And he wants to meet in a public place. Shitty what he did and all, but I'll give him credit for trying to do the right thing today."

Sascha was inclined to agree, but asked Volare and Vish to follow them to the coffee shop all the same. "The sooner we can get this sorted, the better, I think. Otherwise I'll just fuck things up all the more."

Vish pulled the door shut behind them as they left the room, and thumped Sascha on the shoulder lightly with a fist. "Don't go blaming yourself, mink. There was booze, things went sideways. It's not your fault."

Sascha stuffed their hands stubbornly into their pockets and hung their head, then nodded as they made their way to the elevators. "You're right, I'm sorry. I guess I was just worried that I'd chicken out on seeing him again."

Vish grinned, "Wouldn't blame you, but no, this is something that needs talking through before too much time passes, or it'll turn into something ugly."

⋆

Peter met them at the fence of the coffee shop's patio, correctly foreseeing that Sascha would have a hard time making it through the doors if they knew that he was waiting inside.

He didn't hug them, he certainly didn't act out, he didn't do anything but stand with his hands in his pockets and quietly say, "Hi."

"Hi," Sascha offered, at a loss for anything else to say.

"Look, about last night..." He stared at his shoes for a moment before continuing, "I'm sorry. I had too much to drink, and I know that doesn't excuse what I said, just...I'm sorry."

Sascha looked around to find that their friends had backed off and were standing by the entrance. Still within sight, but giving the two privacy.

"It's okay, but maybe we should talk about it," they offered cautiously.

Once inside and at their own table, each with a coffee, both Sascha and Peter seemed to relax. There was the requisite fiddling with condiments, lids, and hot drink sleeves to occupy them and get them used to each other's company in the wake of the previous night, but once seated, there was nothing left to do but talk.

"I'm really sorry," Peter began. He paused for a moment as if to collect his thoughts, then continued. "I can't say I didn't mean to make it about gender, last night. I know we agreed that this would be an experiment, and I can't say yet whether it's passed or failed. I've never been with a guy-" he held up his hand to forestall a response, "I've never been with a guy, not to mention someone like yourself. I think you're wonderful, I really do, but I don't know how to make it work in my head."

They sat in silence, Peter staring down at his coffee lid and Sascha down at their hands. Finally, they dredged up enough words to come up with a reply. "I...don't feel good about last night, but I don't feel bad about this, I guess. I mean, I kind of want to yell at you about that, but I also get what you're saying. I definitely accept your apology, but I need to think a little more about what you said."

Peter nodded and sipped at his coffee, while Sascha's thoughts whirled wildly around their head. They wanted desperately for this thing that they'd been working on for months to work out, but they also wanted to feel safe, not to mention welcome to be who they were. Neither of those things seemed to fit in their mind with what had happened last night.

Finally, speaking slowly, they said, "I know a con breakup isn't what either of us really wanted, but I don't know that this is going to work."

Peter let out a heavy sigh.

"I've got a lot I can say on that, but I don't want to seem like I'm beating around the bush or anything," Sascha continued.

"No, no, I agree," Peter said quietly, clutching at his coffee. "I really want it to, but when I think about you, I think about...I think about my little minky girl, and I just can't make that jive in my head...I don't know what I'm saying."

"Mm, I think I get it, though," Sascha said gently, wary of the bright look of tears in Peter's eyes. "I spent years having it not jive—

'boy this' and 'boy that' didn't work, but neither did anything girly—so here's how I am now."

They drifted back into quiet for a good long while afterward, each watching the room from a different angle as furries bought coffee and early-sermon churchgoers boggled at those in tails and rave gear. They both stayed quiet until each had finished their coffee.

"So," Peter began. "We've got one more day and one more night."

"And everything after."

"And everything after," he agreed.

How Many?

"Oh for pete's sake, quit fretting," Andrew chided, bumping his elbow against Ian's as they crowded into the too-narrow seats. Neither of them were all that skinny anymore, and Andrew was bordering on fat, to Ian's stocky.

Ian closed his eyes and gritted his teeth, focusing on wedging himself in between the window and his boyfriend, counting up slowly through the numbers as he absentmindedly slipped the buckle around his waist.

"Sorry, Ian. I know it's probably harder for you than for me. Like...twice as hard, or was it three times..." Andrew continued, a slight smile twisting the corners of his mouth.

Ian had to smile as well, caving to his partner's wiles and leaning over to place a kiss on his cheek. "I'm just happy you're coming with, really. I can't promise I won't be freaking the whole time, but at least there will be wolves to come back to in the evenings."

Andrew grinned, "Damn right there will! No gallivanting off with weasels for me. Just sitting in the room, twiddling my thumbs, waitin–"

Ian kicked Andrew's foot under the airline seats before settling down against the side of the wall of the plane. "You get plenty of fox time, don't you worry. Rei's there with his whole group of friends. I'm not going to leave you hanging or anything."

"I know, I know. You've told me a few times. I swear you have all your bases covered, just relax and promise me you'll have a good time."

"I'll...I'll try. I promise I'll try."

Ian jumped as there came a steady, barking sound beneath their feet, clutching earnestly at the arm rests as though he might actually leap to his feet, though the plane was taxiing steadily to the runway.

"Hey, hush," Andrew soothed. "Don't worry, it's a normal sound. Just...just make sure you count, and you'll be fine, promise."

Ian nodded. He edged his hands from where they were grabbing at the seat to mock stretch, feeling the sweat coating his palms. Dragging his palms along his jeans from knees to waist, he did his best to calm down and simply let his hands rest, adopting the attitude of someone who wasn't terrified of what was to come, as if that would keep him calm.

It didn't.

Once the engines started to spin up, Ian went rigid, his whole body tensing from head to foot. He deliberately edged his hands back to the armrests, only to find his right hand intercepted by Andrews. Holding gratefully onto both his boyfriend and the plane, he closed his eyes and began counting.

"One, two, three," he mouthed silently, tracing the outline of each number in his mind as he counted up. "Four, five..." The plane began to shake, his eyes went from merely closed to clenched shut.

"Six, seven, eight, nine," he continued, feeling himself sink back into his seat with the acceleration, feeling Andrew's hand getting coated with the sweat from his own. "Ten...eleven..."

"Keep counting," Andrew urged quietly, leaning his bulk toward Ian so that the other could feel the comforting touch all the way from fingertips up to shoulder.

Ian's lips stopped moving, but he kept up the ritual in his head, tracing the numbers, drawing them with a saturated brush on imaginary paper in his mind, from eleven on up. By the time he reached seventy, the plane had gone airborne and made its first little dip after takeoff. By the time he reached one hundred, they were climbing steadily out of Portland International, and he felt more settled than he had during take-off. Just to be sure, however, he began counting once again, starting over at one. It was one of the rules: never count above one hundred.

Andrew, well accustomed to the ritual, relaxed his grip on Ian's hand when he felt him settle down next to him. He knew how much internal strife the anxiety caused, and he knew that it had a half life, decaying exponentially into the ground state, something just slightly more anxious than what he supposed he would consider his own 'normal'. Being a hand to grab as needed was one of the roles he played.

⋆

It took seventeen counts of one-hundred to make it through the flight. The nice part about flying, Ian knew, is that by the time one was at cruising altitude, the plane seemed to morph from a trap into simply a cramped, tube-shaped room. The view out the window turned from horrifying evidence of their speed to something like a tapestry being drawn slowly beneath him. At that point, height seemed to matter less because it was outside his brain's ability to grasp.

The counting came up primarily during take-off, landing, and any turbulence—twice there—as well as the stolid progress of the flight attendants down the aisle-way. They were seated just aft of the wings on this flight, which afforded Ian plenty of time to watch the cart of drinks make its way row by row down the aisle, and he found himself counting—twice again—out of habit as he fretted about what to order to drink, knowing that he'd fail to be understood when the time came.

"Rum-and-coke," he answered, well rehearsed, when the attendant finally made it to him. There was no fall, no muttering or mumbling, nothing exploded, just a quiet response.

The flight attendant accepted his card as he reached past Andrew, knowing that the alcohol would likely calm him in the short term at the expense of the long term.

Andrew knew this too, and murmured to him as his plastic tumbler of ice was prepped, "You sure, hon? I suppose we land late enough we can take it easy..."

"Or stop and get another drink before dinner," Ian joked, accepting the cup, can, and tiny bottle of rum.

Andrew thought for a minute, then shrugged, "We probably could, at that. Vacation Rules."

Vacation Rules meant different things to Andrew than it did to Ian. For Andrew, it meant a relaxation of the stringent ways in which he kept himself, letting the excess that had led to his belly creep into other areas of his life. For Ian, it was another ritual in and of itself, a way to follow up ever action one took with "but we're on vacation" as a means of alleviating the inner tension that went along with his anxiety.

This particular vacation had come with all sorts of extra rules for both of them. Andrew and Ian had made it to plenty of different conventions in the past, both together and separate, but this was the first time both would be going to the same convention with Rei also there. They'd talked through the procedures involved in visiting a shared third partner plenty of times in the past, but only in the last few months had it involved a third partner involved only with one of the two.

It's not that Rei and Andrew didn't get along. They got along fine. They just never seemed to connect on the same level that Rei and Ian had, and they both had seemed happy with that.

Even as Ian counted his way through the plane's choppy descent into Colorado, he felt giddy, as well as nervous. Going through the process of getting close with Andrew, going through the outings-with-friends that slowly turned into dates, had felt natural, but this was something wholly different.

He was going to a Convention! To go on a Date! With someone he *Liked*!

It was all so explicit.

He had only made it up to about thirty-eight or so by the time the plane touched down once more, and was still gripping Andrew's hand in his own. He couldn't stop now, though, so even though Andrew turned to face him, he held up a hand to signal the wait as he made his way through the rest of the numbers before finally settling back into his seat, turning to smile sheepishly at his boyfriend.

"So, um...about that second drink?"

*

The couple managed to make it all the way to the hotel without stopping, despite the rising panic on Ian's part, checking his pockets repeatedly to make sure that he hadn't misplaced his phone, wallet, or keys—the all-important keys with their little vial of emergency pills. No matter how thoroughly he convinced himself that he had everything that he needed, the results would slowly fade into is-it-a-dream-land, and he'd begin questioning his judgement again.

He kept his mouth shut, though, and mostly just clutched at Andrew's hand, letting himself be led to the shuttle, to the hotel, to the front desk, to their room, before finally letting his guard down.

"Hey," Andrew said quietly, resting his hands on Ian's slumped shoulders and guiding him into a hug. "We made it. We don't have to do anything else tonight, except maybe get that drink. That sound good?"

Ian leaned tiredly into the hug, slipping his arms around his boyfriend's waist and holding himself close for a moment, just nodding.

"Need a shower or anything?" Ian asked after a moment.

Andrew shook his head.

Ian nodded and pulled out his phone, quelling the feeling of being sweaty, being caked with sweat, being coated with grime, dirt and grease, grease so thick it showed through his clothes, enveloped them, darkened and then made them translucent, coating him in-

"Ready hon?"

Ian nodded, relaxing his grip on his phone long enough to text Rei to tell him where they would be before stuffing the phone into his pocket. "Yep, let's go," he chirped, striding to the door before

another cycle had the chance to start up.

They made their way down the hallway to the stairs, thankful for the low floor as the elevators were already starting to back up with fur-clad congoers. Elevators were usually okay for Ian, except late at night, and except for glass elevators. Since there would doubtless be late nights at the con and since this hotel had glass-walled elevators overlooking an atrium, they'd specifically requested a lower floor when booking, and had been pleasantly surprised by a room on the second floor.

As they trooped tiredly down the stairs, Ian thought for a moment before pulling out his keys and unscrewing the vial containing his medications.

"Think you'll need that?" Andrew asked.

"Think I already do."

Andrew nodded a little and continued on to the landing before pausing to let Ian catch up.

He carefully split one of the small tablets in half and placed one of the halves beneath his tongue, the learned reaction to the taste bringing an almost immediate sense of calm, however superficial.

"Gonna be okay taking that with a drink?"

"I should be, yeah," Ian responded. "If anything, it'll just make me sleepy, and sleepy is an okay way to be."

Andrew brushed his hand down over Ian's back and nodded, "Well, just keep an eye on yourself. Yap if you need anything."

"Yap!" Ian grinned. "Like that?"

He followed Andrew down the rest of the steps, yapping as he planted his foot on each one. The meds hadn't even started to kick in yet, but he knew they would, and knowing that was enough to lift his spirits to the point where he was actually looking forward to the bar, to seeing Rei.

Rei was shockingly easy to spot at the bar. He wasn't remarkable in his build, but having bleach-blond hair made him stick out in a sea of dark.

"There he is. There he is!" Ian exclaimed and bounded ahead of Andrew. He took the steps up to the bar—a group of two and a group of three separated by a small landing (five was a perfectly acceptable number)—and called out, "Rei!"

The man with the blond hair shot upright and pocketed his phone quickly. "Ast! Is that you?" he asked, meeting Ian—or Ast, as he knew him—in a quick, firm hug. "Jeez, it's good to see you!"

The two regrouped into a more comfortable, less hasty hug, leaning in against each other and simply spending a moment holding tight. The sound of a shutter clicking brought Ian back to attention and he turned his head quickly to see Andrew grinning from behind his phone, holding it up to take another picture.

"H-hey!" Ian stammered.

Rei laughed and grinned, "You must be Andrew. Gonna have to send me those pictures."

Ian felt himself flush, biting back a stinging retort and simply tucking his head back over Rei's shoulder, thankful that they were about the same height. He focused instead on counting. He didn't need a hundred, but he made sure to hold the hug until fifteen. Three and five were particularly auspicious.

Slipping away from Rei, Ian gestured to Andrew, "Um, let me formally introduce you two. Andrew, Rei. Rei, this is Andrew."

They shook hands, then seemed to think better of it and hugged before settling into stools around the bar table, Andrew picking up where Ian left off. "Ast's told me a lot about you, too. Good to finally put a face behind the name. And hey, I like your hair."

"Hah, thanks. Yeah, it feels like I already kind of know you." Rei said, rubbing at the back of his neck. "I uh...I hope it isn't too weird meeting up with your boyfriend's partner. I don't want to...like, impose or anything."

Andrew shook his head and put his hands up disarmingly. "No, trust me, it's fine. We've had this talk so many times just between the two of us, it's good to put it into practice."

The tinkling of glasses breaking behind the group drew their attention, and they turned to see a young woman in paws and a tail rush to clean up a small flood of drink from the table. Ian saw her cut herself on a piece of broken glass, feeling the glass slice into his own flesh within his mind, and winced, swiveling back to face his own table, clasping his hands together in front of himself to keep himself from forcing both Andrew and Rei to turn away, second-hand embarrassment running deep.

Ian had realized how close he was to panicking and had taken the brief, calm interaction between his two partners to clutch at the edge of the table for dear life and work on calming himself. Breathe, slow, calm, chill, breathe. Simple one-syllable words said in order to restore a sense of balance within himself. Finally, he stood, paced in a quick circle behind his chair and shook his hands to dry the sweat from his palms, before settling back onto the stool and grinning sheepishly at Andrew and Rei.

"Sorry," he said breathlessly. "I'm really excited. Um...hi!"

Rei looked a touch taken aback, but Andrew laughed. "Long flight, we're both a little on edge. Seen the waitress around here? I think a drink might do all of us good."

Rei smiled warily, but nodded to someone behind Andrew, catching the eye of the server.

"Help you gents?" the man asked, whisking a cocktail napkin down in front of each of them with practiced ease.

"What beers do you have?" Andrew asked.

The server rattled off a list. The only one that seemed to ring a bell outside of the standard macrobrews was some craft beer, so Andrew ordered that.

Ian tore his gaze off of the table and managed to order a rum and coke. He focused on not fiddling with his napkin too much as Rei ordered a mojito.

Once the server went back over to his station to put in the order, Ian rested a hand on both Andrew's and Rei's knees. Forcing himself into a calmer composure, he smiled between the two of them, "Really glad we could make it, and really good to finally see you, Rei."

Andrew simply smiled back, but Rei leaned in to kiss Ian on the cheek, "You okay there, fox? You seem pretty on edge. Rough flight?"

Ian swallowed hard and quelled the sense of unbalance of only being kissed on one cheek. He focused on the swelling warmth inside his chest, the first sign that the anxiolytics were kicking in. "Uh, well, yeah. I'm just really anxious. Like, most of the time. I'm sorry, it sometimes comes out in strange ways."

Rei reached a hand over and brushed it down Ian's back before resting it on the chair behind him, "No, it's okay! I just wasn't sure what was up, is all."

"I type better than I talk," Ian admitted. "And I talk better if I'm pacing."

Andrew leaned over and knowingly placed a kiss on Ian's other cheek, helping to restore balance, "Hey, don't worry about it, hon. We're all just animals here, no need to worry about how you talk."

Ian was sure that he was blushing red. Bright red, cherry red, fire-engine red, beet red, turning purple, lips blueing, struggling for air, hypoxic. No, none of those. Just blushing, he smiled and gave the knee under each of his hands a gentle squeeze, murmuring, "Just really glad."

Once the drinks arrived, Ian felt that he could relax. The warmth within his chest swelled slowly and was augmented by the addition of the rum in his drink. Conversation eased for him, and he felt himself opening up both to Rei and Andrew. His two lovers shared an occupation as software developers and had plenty to talk about when Ian's stories of online goings-on flagged. He felt comfortable sitting between them, watching someone dressed as a cat flirt with someone who was dressed for something other than the convention, who may not actually have been a part of the convention, but was willing to humor the cat.

Balance became less of a pressing concern as the meds took firmer hold, but even so, as Andrew and Rei chatted about computers, Ian revelled in the feeling of love flowing out from himself and into himself evenly from both sides.

⋆

As the night wore on, through at least two more rounds, Ian settled into a very comfortable spot between Andrew and Rei. The medication he'd taken had filled his head with the softness of cotton and soothed the jagged edges of his anxiety, leaving him feeling almost languid in combination with the alcohol. He contented himself with touching each of his partners, sometimes evenly, sometimes not, enjoying the slight thrill of the lack of symmetry.

By the time he started to feel as though he was nodding, he had his hands entwined with Andrew's and Rei's both.

"Hey, I'm fading, guys," Andrew murmured. He'd always been something of a lightweight when it came to drinking. "Mind if I call it? You two can totally keep up or do whatever."

Rei nodded, "Sure, I've had about my fill of these stools, anyway. Do you...um, do you mind if I steal Ast for a little while?"

Ian felt the blush begin to return as his partners talked about him so plainly.

Andrew laughed, "Sure, go ahead, as long as that's okay with you, hon. You guys should spend some time together."

The blush deepened, but Ian nodded and said, "Yeah, I'd like that. I'll be back tonight, okay?"

Nodding and leaning in to give him a light kiss, Andrew smiled, "You, sir, need to have a good evening, don't fret any. You know where I'll be and how to get in touch. Have fun, you two."

Andrew sauntered off and left Ian with Rei, the both of them sitting in silence for a moment longer.

Finally, Rei offered shyly, "Would you like to head up to the room? Not, like, for anything, just some place quieter? Roommates should be out still."

Ian squeezed Rei's hand in both of his own. "Yeah, let's do that. I'm a little buzzy, and it's a little loud down here."

Rei nodded and moved to settle the tab, covering all three's drinks over Ian's protests, before standing. The two smiled at each other and, before his sleep-, medication-, and alcohol-addled mind had the chance to talk him out of it, Ian stood quickly and leaned to give Rei a soft kiss, more of a smooch than anything.

Rei looked a little startled, but smiled all the wider, slipping his arm around Ian's back and gently guiding him out of the bar, the two talking softly about how good it was to finally have the chance to meet.

"So," Rei said as the door to the room shut behind them. "How'd you and Andrew meet, anyway? I mean, I know how we met..."

Ian laughed and settled onto the bed that Rei led him too, leaning back onto his hands. "We actually met outside of furry, at school. Our campus had a GLBT Student Services office, and we both met there, though I think it only took us a couple of days to figure out that we were both into the furry thing. He's been in it a lot longer than I have."

Rei slipped his messenger bag off of his shoulder and set it down atop a hard-shell suitcase as Ian talked, chatting about how he and Andrew had started dating by default, but found themselves more than compatible.

Rei slipped up onto the bed behind Ian, carefully settling himself on the bed with his legs to either side of his partner's waist. He leaned back onto one of his own hands before carefully drawing Ian toward his front, letting him rest half in his lap, half against his slender front.

Ian fretted for a moment about letting his weight rest against Rei before remembering Andrew's admonition. He had fallen silent when his partner had drawn him close like that, and eventually he managed to relax, murmuring affectionately, "Weasels are slinky."

Rei chuckled and placed a kiss atop Ian's head, replying, "It's in the job description. We can't help it."

Sighing quietly at the kiss, Ian settled both of his hands on Rei's arm around his front and made himself cozy. Everything felt warm, comfortable. There wasn't the same safe feeling he felt with Andrew, but he figured that would come in time. For now, he was content to rest against his lover, asking quietly, "How do you feel about tonight? I hope it wasn't too, you know...awkward."

Rei appeared to think for a moment, then shrugged. "It was good. I mean, I've talked with Andrew some, too, it's not like we don't have anything to talk about or anything."

"But it wasn't weird with me being affectionate with both of you?" Ian fidgeted, "Wasn't weird when I kissed him?"

Rei shook his head. "No. I'm happy to have the time with you now, but I still really enjoyed the evening." He paused for a moment, then asked, "Did the evening make you anxious?"

Ian shook his head drowsily, hiking himself up a little further onto the bed so that he could rest more comfortably against Rei, "Not really, no, just wanted to make sure. I took meds before meeting you in the bar."

Squeezing him a little tighter against his front, Rei nodded silently.

Ian lay for a little bit longer, but eventually sat up, turned to face his partner, and leaned in to kiss him once more, more thoroughly this time. Rei carefully brought both arms up around Ian's shoulders and guided him down to the bed as he lay flat on his back.

Ian shifted up along Rei's front, careful to match movements and stay close. He made sure to set his elbows down to either side of Rei, resting most of his weight on them. The kiss lingered a little longer before parting with the two looking quietly at each other.

"I'm not crushing you, am I?" Ian asked quietly.

"Hush, fox," Rei laughed, taking a cue from Andrew. "Don't fret."

⋆

Ian edged his way as quietly as he could into his room, finding it totally dark.

"Mmm, good evening, hon?" he heard from the blackness, letting the door shut quietly behind him.

Ian nodded before realizing that Andrew wouldn't be able to see him, even if he had his eyes open. "Mmhm, just some cuddling, was nice," he murmured, kicking his shoes off and tugging his shirt up over his head.

"Yeah, you weren't gone all that long."

He blushed at the implication. Had he been gone longer...but no, that was anxiety talking. Anxiety that was growing sharper edged as time went by—the medication was starting to wear thin.

"C'mere, hon," Andrew murmured from the bed. "I'm up now."

Ian slipped out of his pants and down to his briefs, sitting for a moment on the edge of the bed. He could still feel Rei's warmth in his arms by its absence, still catch the faint scent of him in his hair. And yet, here was his boyfriend of the last six years.

Shaking his head to clear the confused tangle of thoughts, he tugged the covers up and slid beneath them alongside Andrew. He leaned in to kiss his partner three times, softly on the lips, before turning his back to him and nestling snug against his front. This is where he belonged. There was belonging with Rei, too, but this is where he was meant to be.

Andrew's arms slipped comfortably around his chest in the dark, pulling Ian warmly against his front, the soft breaths against the back of his neck raising small bumps from there all the way down his arms. "Shh, just relax," came the whispered words against his neck.

Ian did his best to follow his boyfriend's suggestion, settling and relaxing within his grip by conscious effort. Andrew was warm behind him, belly pressed to the small of his back and hips pressed to his backside. He'd apparently been woken during quite the dream as the firm ridge within his boxer-briefs nudging along Ian's rear attested.

He stayed quiet, stayed still, stayed relaxed. This is where he belonged. His own erection strained at the front of his underwear, pent up after an evening of closeness with his other partner and still no release.

One of Andrew's hands wandered sleepily down over his front, brushing over freshly-shaved skin to trace a delicate fingertip along that tented fabric, "Mmm, definitely didn't get up to much, did you, fox?"

Ian melted into his boyfriend's arms and let out a quiet moan. For all his anxiety and all the obsession over being in control, letting Andrew control things completely during sex was one of the only times he could truly let go.

With a deft hand, Andrew hooked both his underwear and Ian's down past their hips in one smooth motion, exposing his own arousal to slip stiffly along his partner's backside. "Wolf wants inside his fox," he growled quietly. "And fox needs his wolf."

The sex was not gentle, though it was quiet, both of them aware of being in a strange room, in a strange bed, and not wanting to make too much noise. After a minute or two of firm grinding, underwear found its way to the floor and the lube had been snagged from the nightstand, and Ian felt himself spread wide by his partner.

The two moved in time, working from a few cautious initial thrusts to a steady rhythm with Andrew holding Ian to his front with one arm while the other hand clutched at his hip, tugging him back to meet his eager thrusts. The feeling was both familiar and titillating. Ian quelled a pang of regret as he felt himself leave streaks of slick precum along the underside of the sheets, the feeling of his erection being dragged across them almost enough to get him off as it was.

Finally, he felt those familiar fingers curl around his shaft and squeeze, stroking shakily as the thrusts became more urgent, less rhythmic. Ian began counting his breaths as they started to catch in his throat. He only made it to twenty-seven before he felt Andrew grind firmly against him from behind and let out a gasp, and only to thirty-three before he felt his own cock pulsing in his boyfriend's hand, waves of pleasure pushing through him and washing any thoughts of numbers out of his mind.

Once his climax had petered down to a dribble within Andrew's hand, Ian let out a long moan and relaxed back against his lover. Andrew had cupped his hand in front of Ian's shaft to catch most of the mess that he'd made, and before Ian could object, he wiped the slick mess up along Ian's clean-shaven front, leaving a smear of seed in a vertical swatch up to his neck. Hands clutched him close, and Andrew growled in his ear, "Marked my fox. You smell of sex, and wolf"

Ian let out a sound, almost a whimper and tensed rigidly against Andrew's front, hands balling up into fists at the combination of erotic teasing and the feeling of being dirty.

"Mine now," Andrew murmured, then leaned in to kiss three

times at the back of Ian's neck. "Go, shower. I know you need to, love."

The rush of relief at being given explicit permission to clean came through as a shudder when Ian relaxed against Andrew's front, pausing for a moment before carefully slipping free of the embrace and turning to kiss him firmly. "Love you," he sighed, very nearly a moan, and slipped out of bed to go clean up.

⋆

Saturday morning started out slowly. Andrew and Ian had spent the hour or so after Ian's shower talking about the night past and hadn't gotten to sleep until late. By the time they made it out of bed, Andrew needed a shower, and Ian felt as though he did too, so they wound up showering together. That ate another hour of time, though Ian felt it was time well spent.

They didn't even really make it out of their room until late in the morning, partly because Andrew kept teasing Ian about the night before, brushing fingertips down over his front right where he'd smeared that slick mess the night before and making Ian squirm at the touch.

This playful attitude kept up all the way down the stairs and out of the hotel before Ian remembered about Rei. There hadn't been any plans around breakfast, though, and he sheepishly left his phone in his pocket. They had all weekend to spend together, and doing something as simple as going and getting coffee with Andrew shouldn't be that big of a deal.

They strolled leisurely through the crowds of begoggled and be-tailed folks in the lobby, making their way out through the doors and down the street to the coffee shop, also visibly filled with the furry crowd. They could spy no less than three tails in the line of five waiting for drinks, and several others who might be congoers as well throughout the seating area.

The settled in a corner table next to a window, Ian keeping his back to the wall so that he could see both out the window and into the room.

"I know I got a little wound up last night, but how was your evening?" Andrew asked, splitting his breakfast burrito in half to let it cool.

Ian blushed and polished his silverware on his napkin, "Not much more than I said, really. Got all cuddly, kissed a little, talked about you and I. It was a good evening."

Andrew laughed and forked bite of burrito into his mouth, nodding and chewing, huffing slightly to cool the bite. "That's good, though. I'm really happy for you," he said, once he could speak again.

Focusing on cutting his burrito into sixteen bite-sized pieces (four was important, but square numbers more so), Ian nodded and took the time to formulate a response. "Yeah. I mean, I feel good about the way things went...er, are going well. I feel really safe with you, and I think I'm learning to feel that way with Rei as well."

Ian tried not to notice as Andrew haphazardly cut off another bite of burrito, "Can you unpack that a little?" he asked. "I mean, I'm glad you feel safe and all, but I...well, I guess I want to make sure you keep feeling that way."

Ian shrugged and nodded, taking the first bite of his burrito and chewing thoughtfully, counting as he went. "I guess, like, it's a two way thing. I feel like I can be myself around you and you accept and work with that, and vice versa. We each have our idiosyncrasies and the other knows how to make...that...work. Sorry."

"For what?"

"I ran out of words." Ian frowned, fumbling over his own thoughts for a moment. "We work with each other, rather than against each other. We don't focus on the thing the other might like, we focus on just being happy, and it works out. I don't honestly know if Rei and I are there yet, but I want to see if we can be,"

Andrew nodded thoughtfully as he chewed on his burrito, washing it down with a coffee drink as he stared out the window. "I think I get it, yeah. It's safe because it doesn't have much friction, and you're finding the way to um....interact with Rei, cold as it sounds, without that friction?"

Ian nodded and worked his way through the first half of his burrito before polishing off a quarter of his coffee. He thought for a moment before adding, "I wish he were here. Rei, I mean. I wish we could all have this conversation together."

"Why didn't you invite him?" Andrew asked, concerned. "He's more than welcome, you know that."

Ian flushed, then rubbed his hands over his cheeks, then his eyes. "I thought about it, I just didn't know if he was awake." The excuse sounded lame, even to his own ears.

"I think it's good stuff, though, have you talked about this with him?"

Ian shook his head and focused on finishing his own burrito in eight smooth motions.

⋆

Rei: Hey, what's up foxy?

Ast: Hi weasel. Sorry I was out most of the morning. At the dealer's den, wanna join?

Rei: In friend's panels. Join later? Dinner?

Ast: Erf, forgot about panels, sorry. Dinner sounds good. Hotel or out?

The lack of reply vexed Ian as he made his way through the Dealer's Den, mentally noting the artists he liked and their positions within the ballroom, planning a future route. He did want to keep up with Rei, this was their time together, but he felt unable to assert himself even enough to ask which panels he was in. He could guess, maybe, by looking at the schedule, but the thought of showing up unannounced presented itself as a jagged corner of anxiety in an otherwise smooth mood.

These corners had been getting out of control, today. It was like some square—or no, some pointed star rotating within him with the points of the corners catching on his soul as though at the hem of a fraying cloth, tugging and pulling at loose threads as he wound his way through the crowds. There wasn't any way for him to keep moving without invoking some ritual or another, whether it was counting to some unattainable number or holding still long enough for his subconscious to catch up.

Ian loathed the fact that there was some sort of medication he needed in order to function within the world around him, and he avoided it at all costs. Cons, or any open, public space, however, seemed to demand such things of him, and there was little he could do to escape it.

"I won't need it," he sub-vocalized. "I can take it later when I can lay down. I won't need it. I can make it through this."

The affirmations had little impact on the part of his brain that kept repeating, "You're visible, you're known, they know you, they can see you, they know how guilty you are, they know what you've done to Rei, how you've betrayed Andrew, they've seen the filth, they know, you're visible..."

He shook his head, trying to clear his mind. It was just the inner critic, he thought, shouting down all the other parts of his personality. He just needed to calm that part of himself, bring the meeting back to order.

Ian found himself standing outside the dealer's den, facing out the windows of the hallway with his hands over his ears.

"I gotta stop," he told the glass. "It needs to stop. I need to stop it."

How he found himself by the elevators, or why, he never knew. Ditto the trip up to the second floor: there was simply no memory of what had happened, beyond the feeling of hands on his shoulders, guiding him out of the tiny box into an empty hallway, limitless placards, hungry doorways.

His mind was filled with numbers. One, two three, four, five six, six...did he get three already? One, two...

"Two...one eight," he repeated to himself. "Two...two nines...two one eight."

The simple math problem calmed him enough to allow him to recognize the placards next to each door before him, and he found himself counting up by twos until he reached the door that proclaimed itself. Two. One. Eight.

Retrieving his wallet was easy, but managing to get the key-card into the slot required to open the door less so. He found himself confronted with a monumental task, weighted down with years of emotion, the actions of his own history, and the incredible importance of what it would mean if he were to open the door. Would they all come tumbling out? It wouldn't mean anything to open the door. It would mean everything if he opened the door.

"Open it," he mumbled, pressing his forehead to the door, eyes angled sharply down to the lock. "Open it."

He slipped the card in. The simple electronic shuffle of the lock cycling was almost a let down. Rei? No. Andrew?

Ian collapsed into the room, the door having provided less resistance than he was expecting. As the door clicked shut, he found himself on all fours, then knees and elbows in front of it. Two. Two nines. Two one eight. Two three four, one two, two times four. Two one eight.

Bed?

The thought was distant, but it seemed to resonate with his elbows and knees. Something something lay down something. The words didn't really line up in his head. Andrew. Rei. The things that made him feel safe. If he could only lay down with Andrew and Rei...

⋆

"Oh jeez, I'm sorry, hon," came the voice from at least a mile away.

"Mmnuh?" Ian asked.

Andrew climbed into bed with his partner, laying on top of the covers before him His hands fumbled down along Ian's sides in search of that key ring with its all-important vial.

"Hot," Ian mumbled. Andrew laughed.

With the key-ring in hand, Andrew unscrewed the vial and fished out a whole tablet of the blessed benzo and, with minimal effort, slipped it into Ian's mouth. "Hey, just relax," he mumbled, leaning up to kiss on Ian's forehead. "Everything's fine, fox, Just relax."

Ian wasn't sure when the blur of torrid panic gave way to simple rest, nor even when his boyfriend's voice really faded in and out, and when it was simple hallucination. He welcomed that cool sensation, though, and sunk down into it.

⋆

Ian woke later that evening to find himself laying down between two sets of hips, the thicker of the two he recognized almost immediately as Andrew's, and on further investigation, he realized Rei was on the other side of him. The TV was playing softly in the background.

"Hey, um," he mumbled, licking his lips to clear the dry mouth that seemed to occupy all of his attention. "Hi."

Both Rei and Andrew smiled down to Ian, and he basked briefly in the glow of their attention.

"Hey," Andrew said. "We got pizza. Just pepperoni. Want some?"

Sitting up in bed made Ian feel the cottony softness that the medications brought to him still filling his mind. He nodded sleepily and accepted a paper plate with a slice of admittedly pretty good-looking pizza from Andrew. He leaned first to the right to kiss his boyfriend on the cheek, then to the left to kiss Rei in the same spot on the other cheek, "Thanks. Um, sorry about all that."

"It's fine!" Andrew promised.

"And sorry I didn't get to see you much until tonight, Rei," Ian offered. "I kinda panicked."

Rei grinned and hugged his arm around Ian's shoulders, "It's okay, really. We've got tonight and the rest of this weekend."

Ian relaxed into his partner's side and focused on eating. Pizza was less than ideal, but it sated the hunger that had cropped up as he slept, though sleep wasn't quite the right word for the fugue of deep anxiety. It was tasty, but simply difficult to decide how best to eat it. He could make it about halfway through with single, even bites, but then had to proceed boustrophedon along the thicker portion of the slice until he got to the crust, which he could break up into four pieces and eat one at a time.

Knowing that he wasn't up for leaving the room again that night, Ian settled into bed between his two partners. Watching TV at a convention wasn't really what anyone wanted, but being able to spend time with loved ones was certainly worth it. They managed to find some movie to leave on quietly in the background and settled in to talking, then into cuddling, with Ian feeling safe between Andrew and Rei.

As the night went on, the trio slipped further down into bed until they were lying flat, Rei spooning up behind Ian with his arms wrapped around him, Ian hugging those arms to his front as he nuzzled and kissed with Andrew.

As the cuddling grew in intensity and sensuality, Rei bit gently down on Ian's shoulder, right where it met with his neck, getting a quiet moan out of his partner.

"Uh-oh," Andrew grinned. "You found one of his buttons. Keep it up, and make sure to get the other side, too."

Rei held his grip a little longer before kissing at that spot, then along the back of Ian's neck, to bite gently on the other shoulder.

The fact that both of his partners were taking control of him in such a way had Ian blushing bright red, not least of which because he was also intensely aware of his arousal, as well as that of Rei pressed firmly to his backside. The gentle biting continued along his shoulders and neck as Rei pressed firmly to him with a gentle rocking motion.

Andrew shifted some in front of Ian, slipping one hand down to cup over his boyfriend's tented jeans as he reached back with the other to snag the plastic bag that held the condoms and bottle of lube they had brought along to the con. The biting on his neck stopped as Rei looked up, curious.

Ian's eyes widened, "H-hey..."

"Shh, it's okay, just relax, fox," Andrew murmured, passing the bag over Ian to Rei, who took it cautiously. "You two should have some fun, it feels like you're already on your way."

Ian chewed on the inside of his cheek for a moment, then nodded. "Can you...can you stay? Is it alright if he stays, Rei?"

Andrew thought for a moment, then nodded, "I'll stay if you want, if it's okay with Rei."

Rei had been quiet throughout the exchange, holding himself still against his partner and clutching the plastic bag in one hand. "Um...If you'd like, sure. I'll admit I've never done anything in front of someone else, much less my partner's partner."

Ian felt flustered, but clutched one hand on either of his partners, unable to meet either of their gaze. His blush seemed to be consuming his face with its heat, but he could feel his shaft pulsing stiffly against Andrew's hand still lingering on his crotch.

After a few more moments of stillness and silence, Ian worked up the courage to stammer, "T-take your fox?"

Rei let out something akin to a quiet growl and gave another firm grind of his hips to Ian's, biting down on his shoulder once more, more firmly this time, before rolling free to extract a condom and the lube from the bag. Andrew did his part in helping by unfastening the button to Ian's pants, slipping the zipper down and helping his boyfriend scoot both pants and briefs down to his knees, freeing his erection from the confines.

Leaving himself mostly clothed as well, Rei managed to unroll the condom down along his own shaft and coat it thoroughly with the slick lube. That accomplished, he rolled himself back to face Ian, leaning away from him enough to peer down his front as he worked the tip of his cock up against, then very carefully into his lover.

Ian, for his part, clutched tightly to Andrew, burying his face against his boyfriend's shoulder and letting out a soft moan as he felt Rei slide into him. Rei felt thinner inside of him than Andrew did, but longer as well, and the whole experience was almost jarring, in a pleasant sense. He felt connected, emotionally and physically, to both of the people he treasured most.

Edging himself forward until his hips were pressed firmly to Ian's bare backside, Rei let out a shaky breath. He slid his hands up under Ian's shirt and inched the fabric up until he could help his partner out of the garment, breaking his grip on Andrew only momentarily.

Thus exposed, he dragged his fingernails down over the skin of Ian's back, grinning as the back arched to the touch.

As they relaxed, the two settled into a slow and comfortable rhythm. Ian rocked gently with each of Rei's thrusts into him as he held his upper body close to Andrew. Rei, confident in the red scratch-marks along Ian's back, settled his hands on his partner's hips to hold them still as he moved within him. Andrew contented himself with kissing gently along Ian's forehead while his hands busied themselves with his boyfriend's own stiff arousal, caressing along it in time with the thrusts.

Ian focused on counting along with his breaths. He made it a point during sex to breathe steadily and evenly. Four counts in, hold for one count, four counts out, hold for one count. He knew that the definition of a 'count' changed as he got more worked up, but it was important that he remain consistent.

They didn't speak much, and the TV was too low to make make out, and so the only sounds were the gentle sounds of sex: quiet affirmations, gentle rustling, and the occasional sound of Rei's hips meeting up with Ian's rear after a particularly hard thrust. Andrew coaxed Ian on with gentle cooing, while Rei murmured, "My fox," under his breath.

The feeling of belonging, of being taken by both his partners in a way, touched Ian both emotionally and physically. Usually, it took him longer to get off than Andrew, but tonight, his body seemed to rush toward climax. He didn't even have a chance to count his breaths before he felt the familiar surge of pleasure, spurt after spurt of his cum coating Andrew's hand, wrist, and front.

"Mmm, goodness," Andrew murmured into his ear. "There you go, good fox..."

Ian whimpered and shivered through his orgasm, tilting his head up to kiss Andrew firmly on the lips, something he couldn't easily do during climax in their usual set of positions.

Rei, sensing his partner's climax, redoubled his efforts, picking up the pace of his thrusts and clutching all the more firmly at Ian's hips. It didn't take too much longer—only twelve more shaky breaths by Ian's count—before Rei pressed himself firmly forward one last time, leaning forward to bite down on Ian's shoulder as pleasure overtook him.

Spent, the partly clothed couple simply held themselves still and worked on catching their breath. Ian could feel Rei's chest heaving against his back beneath the soft fabric of his t-shirt, reveling in the comfort of being held twice over as he rested his head back down against Andrew's chest.

"Mmm, two good animals," Andrew hummed softly, holding himself still as his boyfriend relaxed into calmer breathing and relaxation.

Ian held himself still as long as he was able. The corners of his anxiety were starting to make themselves felt once more, spurred on primarily by the sensation of his semen starting to cool in the room's air, making him feel coated and dirty. Even so, it was nice to be held by both partners and share in the moment while he could.

Finally, the need to be clean overrode the coziness, and he murmured quietly, "I need to go get cleaned up, can I get up real quick?"

Rei peeked questioningly over Ian's shoulder to Andrew who nodded his assent. Both of them disentangled from their lover and let him slip carefully out of bed and shuck his pants the rest of the way before making his way off to the bathroom.

"...just needs to be clean, nothing wrong..." Ian overheard Andrew explain before he shut the door, keeping his embarrassment to himself as he started the water running for the shower.

A scant minute or so later, he heard the door to the bathroom open. Someone washed their hands thoroughly followed by a bulk settling onto the closed lid of the toilet. Peeking out from behind the shower curtain, he saw Andrew sitting there, rubbing his face in his hands.

"You okay, wolf?" Ian asked quietly, soaping his hands up for another round of trying to clean himself of the slick lube.

"Yeah. I'm okay. I don't know if that was really what I needed, but I'm happy for you."

Ian stood in silence for a moment until he was done soaping and rinsing. Finally, he replied, "I'm sorry, I just...I just wanted you both there, I guess. It was very nice to feel."

"Yeah, no, I get that." Andrew sighed, "You're just my fox, you know? I could accept you and Rei as an intellectual thing before now, but that just kind of made me internalize it...a little more forcefully than I was expecting."

Ian nodded and ran his hands down over his body, checking for any hint of slickness from lingering spots of lube before realizing that Andrew couldn't actually see him. Rather than replying right away, he shut the water off and grabbed a towel, drying himself in the tub. Once he was mostly dry, he folded the towel neatly in quarters and slid the shower curtain back, laying the folded towel on the floor in front of the toilet before daintily stepping out.

"I'm your fox, wolf, and nothing's ever going to change that," he murmured, settling himself down onto his knees and resting his hands on his partner's knees. "You and Rei play different roles in my life, and nothing is supplanting anything that was there before."

Andrew nodded and took one of Ian's damp hands in his own and smiled tiredly. "Promise?"

"Promise," Ian murmred, leaning up to kiss his partner on one cheek, then the other. He stood to dry the rest of the way with a smaller towel.

"Hey Ian?"

"Yes, wolf?"

Andrew paused for a moment. "How many? How many roles do you think you need filled?"

Ian draped the smaller towel around his shoulders and thought for a second. "I don't have an answer for that, hon. I just know you're the first, and will always be."

Andrew stood again, level with Ian so that he could kiss him gently on the lips. "And you'll always be my fox?"

Ian nodded, smiled.

"Come on, then," Andrew rumbled. "I left Rei out there to clean up. Thanks for yapping, though."

"Yap!"

Andrew smiled, more earnestly this time.

Ian let Andrew precede him out of the bathroom. He thought for a moment, smiled, and hung up his towel. Anxiety quelled, he headed back out into the room, to both his partners.

Again

Michael woke blearily to the sounds of muffled giggling, rubbing the sleep from his eyes and lifting his head off the pillow. He couldn't quite make out what was going on in the bed next to his own, but it appeared to be quite fun, or at least funny.

Rooming with his friends came with its benefits, but also its drawbacks. No one had been particularly shy about the fact that part of the reason they had come to the convention in the first place was to play around and get laid, and that was just sort of part of the bargain when it came to rooming with others. He smiled slightly that it was those two who had started messing around before he and his own bed-mate had; he knew Bomber had quite the crush on him.

On that note, he rolled over in bed, putting the giggling behind him, and slipped his arm around the still sleeping Bomber. He fit snuggly behind the slightly smaller form, doing his best not to rouse his friend, content for the moment just to enjoy the shared warmth of laying close to someone. Bomber, for his part, simply mumbled something incomprehensible and appeared to go right back to sleep, comfortable against Michael's front.

He apparently dozed off, because the next time he woke up,

the giggles had been replaced with muffled panting and the quiet, rhythmic rustle of...it couldn't be much more than a blow job, given that only the blankets seemed to be rustling, rather than the entire bed.

"Morn'," mumbled Bomber.

"Shh, quiet," Michael whispered, confirming his hunch with a look over his shoulder. "Very important things happening over there."

There came a laugh from the other bed, along with a muffled giggle. "Very important, verrrry warm," Alexis replied, voice slurring with the effort of enunciation while receiving oral sex.

Michael rolled slowly onto his back and canted his head to watch the goings on, while Bomber sleepily rolled over next to him and rested his head on Mike's shoulder.

They couldn't see Corrin, and with as skillful as he seemed to be, could barely hear the fox moving rhythmically beneath the covers, except for the rustle of blankets on hair.

Skillful indeed. Before too much longer had passed, Alexis' eyes shot open and his jaw dropped, breath catching in his throat only to be let out in a hasty, "Oh fuck." Alexis shuddered, Corrin drastically slowed his movements, and Michael and Bomber looked on in appreciation.

"Mmm, well done, you two," Michael offered, getting a breathy giggle from Alexis and a grin from Bomber, whose own hand was inching its way down over his front, seemingly casually but obviously aiming for the crotch.

Both Michael and Bomber had slept only in their underwear, and watching the little show did have Michael somewhat worked up, so he tolerated the touches—tentative at first, then a little more exploratory over the tented boxer-briefs that he wore—though it felt a little awkward with Bomber. He knew how much he meant to his friend, but considering him only a friend, felt he had little he could offer that would satisfy him. He tended towards women, usually, but wasn't above the friendly touch.

Corrin slunk from under the covers with a sheepish grin on his face, muttering, "Hi, guys." He kissed Alexis on the cheek, took the other's hand in his own, and guided him out of bed. "C'mon, let's grab the shower first."

Alexis nodded and managed to slip out of bed behind his friend, tugging his discarded boxers along after him and using them to cover his crotch, walking quickly behind Corrin, who was doing his best to hide his own erection.

"Have fun," Bomber offered.

"Yeah, and save some hot water for the rest of us."

Michael and Bomber settled comfortably back into bed, Bomber nestled in against Mike's side as he continued to pet gently along his friend's flagging arousal, his own pressed firmly to Michael's hip. After a silence, he asked, "This okay, Roo?"

Michael nodded, eyes closed.

Another long silence, then, "Can...can I do any more?"

Michael hesitated a bit. There was no denying that the touches felt good, but that lingering sense of awkwardness remained. "Um...no. Not this time, maybe soon?" he offered.

Bomber nodded, abashed, and settled himself back against Michael's side. The touches slowed, but continued, more carefully than before, lest they cross a boundary. Eventually, they settled to a stop, and Bomber simply slipped his arm around Michael to hug himself closer, murmuring, "This is good, too."

Michael nodded in agreement to that, brushing his hand up along Bomber's back to hug around his shoulders, helping to keep his friend warm against him while they waited on their own turns at the shower. It would be a bit, yet.

⋆

Saturday morning—nearing afternoon by the time Michael, Bomber, Alexis, and Corrin drew the curtains and made it out of the room—was a pleasant affair. The four made their way to a nearby coffee shop, managing to pick up two more along the way: a lion and his intensely shy friend who looked to be some sort of blue fox or wolf, if the tail was anything to go by.

They shared coffee and gossip, laughter at the expense of Alexis and Corrin, and the Shy Blue Fox produced a clipboard with paper from his messenger bag and polled everyone for their species and began sketching.

Michael, from his position next to the Shy Blue Fox, watched the sketch take shape. He wasn't much of an artist, himself, but always found it fascinating to watch artists work, turning what looked like the simplest of shapes into something that carried meaning.

"Is that you, Roo?" he heard a husky voice from behind him, feeling crossed arms settle onto the back of his chair.

Michael turned quickly. Something about the voice tickled his memory in strange, not altogether unpleasant ways. A short man with a well-kept goatee stood back upright behind his chair, crossing his arms over his chest and smiling down to Michael.

"So it is."

"Do I know..." Michael began, half rising out of his chair.

It was the height that tipped him off, more than anything. The skin was rougher, the hair cut from waist-length to a sort of unisex pixie cut, the facial hair, the masculine, well-built chest. There was something about how this person was exactly the same height as...

"Glade! Holy shit, is that you, Glade?"

The other man nodded, then bust into a wide grin, uncrossing his arms and holding them open in an invitation to a hug. Michael stood fully from his chair and moved cautiously into to the hug, wrapping his arms firmly around Glade for a good long moment before stepping back once again to look over him. The hug felt familiar, and yet incredibly different at the same time.

"You look...ah...very different," was all he could manage.

Glade laughed easily, tossing his head to clear the hair from in front of his eyes. "That's an understatement. What do you think?" he asked, standing a little taller.

Michael couldn't quite keep his mouth from hanging open, much less form any words. "I...you...well you look good! You'd always talked about...but I didn't think..."

Glade kept grinning, reaching forward to pat Michael gently on the cheek, "Don't worry, don't need to think too hard. I'm doing things that make me happy. I won't pester you too much, I just wanted to say hi. It's been, what, five years?"

Michael struggled to define what he was feeling, the violent mix of old emotions combined with the surprise of seeing Glade after so long. All he could do is nod.

The two stood in silence for a moment longer before Glade reached to give Michael's bicep a squeeze, "Well, it's good seeing you. I'll let you get back to it, maybe see you around?"

Michael nodded and croaked, "See...see you."

When Glade sauntered off and he turned back to the table, he found everyone staring up at him silently. Alexis was the only one who had known Michael long enough to know of the stormy end to his relationship with Glade. It had been kept behind closed doors for the most part, except for one notable exception, to which Alexis had been witness and help Michael clean up the blood from his broken nose.

"Sorry," he mumbled awkwardly. "Old friend. Ex."

The corners of Alexis' mouth twitched up slightly into a smile.

Bomber, sitting on the other side of Michael from the Shy Blue Fox, rested a hand on his knee and gave it a gentle squeeze beneath the table. "You okay? Look kinda shocked."

Michael nodded and scooted the last few bites of his breakfast burrito around on his plate before giving up and wrapping his hands around his coffee cup and leaning back in his chair.

"Yeah, it's just a bit of a shock. We were only together for a year and a half or so, but she...uh, he now, I suppose, cut contact after a bit of a messy breakup. It's just a surprise."

"Been a long time then?"

Michael nodded once more, "Yeah, about five years or so, I think. Sh- he, I mean, had always talked about gender and stuff, didn't really think they'd...change."

Rubbing his hand on Michael's thigh comfortingly, Bomber nodded. "That'd be a big shock, I guess."

Michael relinquished his coffee mug to rub his hands over his face before patting at Bomber's own on his leg. "Jesus. Yeah. It's...not bad, of course, I'm happy for...him, but I think I just need to think about it for a bit."

Michael kept quiet through the rest of the brunch with his

friends. Bomber lost interest before long and went back to talking with Corrin and Alexis. The lion had been edging closer to the Shy Blue Fox, and eventually seemed to cave and just rest his head down on the other's shoulder. watching the lazy sketch session. The Shy Blue Fox hadn't said more than a handful of words through the whole morning, but the lion didn't seem to mind. Con love, Michael thought.

It took them longer than Michael would've liked to make it out of the coffee shop. He hadn't successfully worked through the mess of thoughts and emotions surrounding seeing Glade, and so different now, at least not enough to make it back into the conversation. However, the hard wood of the seat hadn't let him relax at all, and so he'd been antsy as he alternated between wandering through old memories of his mistress (master?) and watching the Shy Blue Fox finish up his sketch with firmer strokes of his mechanical pencil. It was a little cartoonish for Michael's taste, but he'd muttered his appreciation and thanks as the Shy Blue Fox tugged the sheet of paper from the clipboard and skimmed it to the middle of the table.

Eventually, a critical moment seemed to be reached when enough people decided that they were done and started clearing up paper cups and clinking plates to bring to the trash and dish drop. Michael looked cautiously around himself before breathing a sigh of relief when Glade was no where to be found. He scraped the uneaten bites of his burrito into the garbage and set his place along the growing stack above the trashcan before following his friends out into the sun and warmth.

They trundled back to the convention hotel before all seeming to split and go their separate ways. Alexis made his way to the art show to bid on a piece he'd heard would be in it. Corrin followed for a few yards before getting intercepted by a friend of his and dragged into a growing conversation circle. Bomber gave Michael a questioning look before heading off to the Dealer's Den to see if, luck of all luck, they had a mouse tail for him. The lion and the Shy Blue Fox drifted down the hallway, away from the hubbub of the central lobby to, presumably, make out some more.

Michael stood for a few moments, finally free of the burden of conversation so that he could think about what had just happened. Glade had always been...

He shook his head to pull himself out of his reverie. He was staring into space like some lunatic. He forced his feet to move, carrying him toward the bank of elevators that would take him back to his room. He did need to think, but he certainly didn't need to do so in the lobby.

He wound up sharing the ride up with a gryphon in suit (which took up most of the back of the elevator, and a skittish, stocky fellow who pressed the button for two, then spent the entire short ride with his palms pressed firmly over his eyes. When the door opened and he didn't move, Michael gently guided him out of the elevator and received a mumbled, "thanks."

Michael shrugged to the gryphon and hit the door closed button. The gryphon shrugged back, exaggerated in suit.

Three floors up, Michael made his way out of the elevator, giving the silent fursuiter a wave before trodding off to his room.

Housekeeping had obviously been through the place, replacing glasses, cleaning the bathroom. He poured himself a rum and coke on a whim—it was a con, after all—then flopped down onto one of the freshly made beds and clasped his hands over his front, staring up the ceiling.

There hadn't been a huge, prolonged break-up; just a rough month of small spats and then the crushing argument wherein they had realized that they knew each other less well than they had originally thought. That was when Glade had spilled her—no, his—heart out about the ways in which gender intersected with his life, their relationship, and his sexuality. Michael had been dismissive, and it hadn't gone over well.

"You get only what you deserve, roo," Glade had growled, punched him in the face, and, minus a few curt emails, that had been the last either had seen of each other.

⋆

Michael felt the warmth of the rum-and-cokes he'd had up in the room starting to fill him by the time afternoon slid into evening and he made his way down to the bar. There was something cathartic, in a way, drinking to old memories. It didn't necessarily resolve anything, but the alcohol could let you pretend that it had. At least now he felt more able to take in the fact that he would be, in a way, sharing this convention with Glade. After all, not all of the memories were unpleasant.

The elevators ejected him into a lobby more packed with people than it had been before, filled with hundreds of missed connections. He made his way languidly through the crowd, scanning faces, scanning badges, handing out smiles. It felt good.

"Oh hey, it's you guys!"

The lion and the Shy Blue Fox looked up from where they were trying to share a seat in one of the lobby's chairs, one earbud in each of their ears leading to a phone held by the Shy Blue Fox. They looked up to him slowly, smiled with recognition and reached hands out to grab him in for an awkward hug. Not sober, but maybe not necessarily drunk, the two seemed more alive and active than they had earlier in the day.

The three of them decided on the hotel restaurant as a good source of dinner. Expensive, but fitting for three innebriated furries to chill and at least get food in the system before the evening's dances began. They settled into a booth and ordered a round of drinks, beers and a gin and tonic.

"So," Michael began, putting what he had hoped was a conspiratorial tone in his voice. "Good day for you two?"

The Shy Blue Fox buried his face in his hands and giggled, while the lion looked serene. "Mmm, yeah, very good. Bit of molly, lots and lots and lots of hugs."

Michael laughed out loud. Colorado wasn't exactly the heart of Ecstacy, but it showed up every now and then. More common now was marijuana—legalization had played a roll in a good number of the attendees showing up here, he was sure.

"Good, glad you guys are having a good time."

The lion looked almost beatific as the Shy Blue Fox rubbed himself almost sinuously up against him, reveling in the touch.

"How about you, man?" the lion asked. "Been a good con so far?"

Michael nodded distractedly and sipped at his water, "Good enough, yeah."

"Saw your...your ex? Saw your ex showed up, earlier."

"Yeah, I was surprised to see...them here. I wasn't expecting that."

The lion cocked his head, "Been a long time?"

"Yeah, definitely. Five years or so."

"Not a pleasant break up?"

"Yeah she...she at the time, broke my nose and we vowed to never see one another again."

"But you hugged-" the Shy Blue Fox began.

Michael brushed it off with a wave of his hand. "Yeah. There's a lot there," he stammered, searching for the words. "Plenty of good memories, along with the bad. It's good to see her. Him. It's good to see him."

Ecstasy, in his own experience, added quite a bit to the level of empathy one normally had, and often led to picking up on cues that were embedded in day to day speech, bits of meaning that exposed more despite all attempts to hide. It was no different with these two.

"He's not what you were expecting. Quite the change, huh?"

Michael felt his face flush, and looked down toward the table, nodding.

There was a silence that stretched until their drinks arrived, thankfully not too long.

Finally, the Shy Blue Fox asked, "Do you think you'll see him again, during the con? Like...actively?"

Michael hid his face in his beer, sipping slowly to buy himself time. "Maybe." He set his beer down and twisted the glass between his fingers. "Maybe."

⋆

By the time Michael made it to the dance, he was decidedly buzzy, full of rum and coke, beer, and mediocre pizza from the hotel kitchens. It was fuel enough for fucking around in the dance, he figured. Not like anyone was likely to notice his un-fursuited form stomping away on the ballroom floor to deep house or yacht punk or whatever the hell kids were spinning these days.

The dance was a just good way to let loose. For him and so many others.

He prowled down the long hallway from the hotel restaurant to the ballroom, weaving skillfully between clumsy fursuiters and those moving much slower than he.

He felt good. Real good. This had been a good day overall, from watching his friends have their fun in the morning, all the way down to dinner. Even, he admitted to himself, seeing Glade again, in all his newfound confidence.

The dance was packed, even for as early as it was. Saturday was one of the two big nights, with a line-up of two-hour DJ sets that lasted nearly until dawn, and programming had stopped hours ago. So it was to be expected that there would be a ton of people there, Michael thought, showing his badge to the guard at the door and bouncing in time with the thumping music even as he made his way into the ballroom, quickly picking up the time as he moved.

The music washed over him, thick as honey, as he moved out onto the floor. It pushed at him, tugged at him, guided his movements between the furries out on the floor, both in and out of suit. He knew he wasn't a graceful dancer, or even a good one, but he couldn't deny how good it felt to move along with the beat.

It was some uncounted number of songs later before he noticed the form moving closer to him, hips swaying in the rhythm of the music through the crowd. He was sweating, and he could feel dinner's two drinks coursing through his veins, that was about the only indicator he had that it was later on in the evening.

Glade.

He slowed his movements, settled down into a relatively quiet sway where he stood on the dance floor, watching as Glade moved up to him through the crowds. The presumed hormone therapy had changed the shape of his previous mistress, shifting the bulk of his weight up toward his middle and away from his hips, and what had been a generous bosom had been drastically reduced—how, he couldn't say. The walk had changed too, though not in any way he could pinpoint. More movement to the shoulders, perhaps.

What he saw, stalking toward him rhythmically through the crowd of dancing furries, was a well-built, clean young man, dressed in jeans, a skin-tight shirt, and a leather jacket, who somehow still retained so many recognizable features of his old partner.

Glade reached out and took his hand, drawing him dancingly from the floor and away from the speakers to the back of the room. Michael followed helplessly, half in awe and half in shock at his former mistress' directness.

They both moved subconsciously to the beat, shifting their hips and their weight in time with the music, then nearly pausing as the beat built up to the drop.

Glade brought him to an unoccupied section of the wall at the back of the ballroom and turned him firmly so that his back was to the wall, then pressed him up to it. He seemed deliberate in his actions, making sure that Michael's back was flat against the wall before planting his hands surely beneath each of his arms, leaning in close to him. He had to stretch up a little in order to make himself heard as he spoke quietly.

"Lets have some closure here, roo."

Michael swallowed roughly at the sure signs of dominance that remained in his ex's actions. "What," he began, and swallowed once more. "What sort of closure do you want?"

"One more night," Glade murmured. "Tonight, you're mine, we

take what we had at the best of times, and have that be the end, and we go back to being comfortable friends, rather than what we had before."

"But you're-"

"I'm me, and all you need to be is my little pet roo, just once more."

Michael swallowed hard once more, keeping his hands flat against the fabric of the dividing wall behind him. The alcohol, the dominance, the familiarity all worked in Glade's favor, and he couldn't do much to suppress the excitement that had lingered since that violent outburst that had ended their relationship in the first place.

All he had to do was reconcile that it was really over, and on agreeable terms.

He felt dizzy, looked up to find no relief in the swirling lasers and lights that projected from the stage, a glowing arachnid of greens, blues, and purples.

"T-tonight," he stammered, "I'll be your little pet roo."

The grin that creased Glade's face was knowing, pleased, with maybe a touch of evil. The music began to rise once more in a crescendo.

"You're already a little buzzed, I can smell the beer." Glade held up a slender tube which tapered to a small mouthpiece and glowed with a blue LED, "Will you still be my good little pet if I get you a little more buzzed?"

It took Michael a moment to understand what was being offered. Once he figured out the vape pen, he nodded shakily. Glade knew him through and through, knew how much he liked placing himself into someone else's hands. Glade took the nod as assent and tilted the mouthpiece of the vape to his lips, not yet pressing the button that activated the heating coil.

"You'll be my pet?"

Michael nodded.

"You'll please your dom?"

Michael took in the new term, nodded.

"I've got my crop."

Michael flushed in the dark, nodded.

"Do you have your paws with you?"

Another nod.

"Same safeword. 'Rouge'?"

Michael squirmed between Glade and the wall, nodded once more.

Glade pressed down on the stud that activated the vape and pressed the tip of it between Michael's lips, quietly instructing, "Breathe in. Slow."

Michael knew the theory behind the devices, and so he breathed in slowly and carefully, tasting the not-quite-smoke flavor of pot on his tongue and down his throat, flowing liquidly within him and filling him with both a sense of fullness-of-being and hunger that he couldn't quite put his finger on.

The devices were frowned upon by the hotel, no matter what they contained, so Glade kept the LEDs covered by his finger and palm, letting Michael have a good long inhale before swiftly pocketing the vape once more.

Michael held the warm vapor for a few seconds, then let it out with a few gentle coughs, muffling the sound as best he could.

"Come on," Glade said, with a sudden, earnest smile. "Let's finish this set, at least."

The two moved back out onto the dance floor.

Michael felt the pot take him over in a matter of minutes, rolling in from his extremities until he felt as though he was dissipating into a cloud. The music moved through him with such ease, and he felt like some luminous being, moving against and with the other luminous being of Glade, enjoying both the space and tension between themselves, as well as the friction of cloth on cloth or leather as they brushed up against one another.

Some unknown amount of time later, the set drew to a close amid the cheers of their fellow dancers, and Michael and Glade drifted from the dance floor, hand in hand, out past the guard and into the hallway.

Michael found it difficult to stop dancing, swaying gently from side to side and rocking his weight back and forth even as they made their way over to the bank of elevators. Glade laughing at him was all he needed in terms of encouragement. He got the impression that Glade himself wasn't entirely sober, and he felt in good company—comfortable, like how he used to feel when they smoked together.

They made their way to the elevators and stood with a tired looking canine suiter and a few other up-late furries, waiting.

Glade leaned in against his arm and tugged him down a little closer, murmuring, "Your room okay?"

Michael nodded. The whole room had agreed to let private liaisons be allowed, and so anyone who was there and not already in the middle of something should agree to clear out if Michael needed.

The ride up was uneventful, and likewise opening the door into an empty room. Alexis was probably still dancing with Corrin, and Bomber was probably hovering around the edges of the dance, unsure of where he belonged.

Michael slipped into the room with Glade, then bent down to offer a kiss, falling back into old habits with the drink and pot filling him with warmth. Glade leaned up to meet the kiss, but quickly took Michael's lower lip between his own and bit down on it. He tugged carefully downward until Michael's face was level with his own before letting up on the bite. "You going to be a good pet tonight?"

Michael sucked his lower lip into his mouth and searched briefly for the taste of blood before nodding bashfully, "I'm going to be a good pet."

"Strip, then," Glade ordered imperiously. "And get your paws on."

Michael hesitated, swaying a little on his feet. Glade reached behind his back and extracted a small riding crop from his back pocket, simply holding it at his side.

Michael got the hint, and slipped over to where his bag lay next to the bed, fishing out his paws: gloves of dark brown faux fur. He moved back to where Glade stood and carefully slipped out of his shirt and tugged his jeans and underwear off, standing exposed and erect in front of Glade. He shivered slightly in the air-conditioned room, though at least half of that was due to his excitement.

"Now me," Glade ordered quietly, holding his arms out.

"Yes mistr-" Michael began, before realizing his mistake. He winced as Glade raised the crop, then braced himself and held still. There was a quick crack and an almost satisfying sting against the left cheek of his buttocks.

"You will call me Dom Glade, little pet," he purred. "No more slip-ups."

"Yes...Dom Glade," Michael whispered. The strike had hurt initially, but with his body buzzing in its high, the sting was quickly turning into the familiar pleasant sensation they had experimented with so long ago.

Glade held his arms out and let the naked Michael slip the leather jacket off, then lifted his arms for Michael to lift his shirt. There was something intimate about undressing his former partner, even having been ordered to do so, and he took his time, being mindful of the crop.

Beneath his shirt, Glade was bare, no binder or anything. There were just two well-healed scars, each curving gently beneath his nipples, where the mastectomy had taken place. Michael brushed his hands, fuzzy in their paws, softly down over his ex's chest, wonderingly. There was so much more body hair than he had remembered, more than some of his roommates here at the con, come to think of it.

"There you go, little roo," Glade murmured, sounding pleased. "You're halfway there. Kneel to do the rest."

Michael nodded and obediently lowered himself to his knees, reaching up with his paws to work on unfastening the button of Glade's jeans, fumbling partly because of the fake fur and partly out of nerves and excitement. Glade wore boxers—though he always had—which slipped part way off his hips as his jeans were carefully tugged lower.

Michael reached his fur covered hands up to rest just above the wasteband of Glade's pants and underwear, uncertainty growing within him. He finally smoothly slid his hands down, taking the garments along with them to free his ex from his pants. He hadn't been sure what to expect, seeing that Glade had opted for top surgery, but found himself confronted with the neatly trimmed crotch that still felt familiar to after all these years.

Glade chuckled quietly above him, drawing the tongue of his crop up along Michael's back to tease gently across his shoulders. "Expecting something different, little pet?"

Michael flushed and drew his hands lightly up over Glade's legs once more, the fur of the gloves brushing through the hair of his ex's body. "I...don't know what I was expecting."

Glade tapped the leather tongue of the crop gently against the back of Michael's head, "I'm comfortable how I am. I can present how I like, and little pets can still worship me."

His cheeks still red, Michael nodded and swallowed, carefully rehearsing in his arousal- and drug-addled mind what he was going to say next. "May I worship you, Dom Glade?"

Glade walked slowly around Michael as he sat, kneeling and aroused on the floor. He seemed intent on drawing the moment out and letting Michael stew. The tongue of the crop kept tapping and prodding, as though it were inspecting all the ways in which his body had changed over the years. The process of waiting had that flavor of delightful agony that Michael knew Glade was keen on.

Finally, Glade relented and sat back on the edge of the bed behind Michael, tapping him gently on the shoulder with the crop before leaning back onto one of his hands. "There's a dam in one of the pockets of my coat. Get that, and you may worship me."

Michael tried not to appear too eager as he crawled over to the crumpled jacket and tugged out the plastic-wrapped dental dam. Aside from a few instances of almost fooling around, like that morning, he had been mostly abstinent throughout the last five years, and he lept at the chance to service his old owner as he used to (with that bit of latex in between, this time—they weren't fluid-bonded anymore). It might be the alcohol and pot buzzing through him, but he felt right, in his place.

Glade kept his noises primarily to purrs and growls, huskier than Michael remembered. Even so, the act maintained its familiarity to him: the long teasing licks, the shorter feathery ones, lazily spelling his name out in cursive against the latex of the dam before delving a little more adventurously between the labia of his former—and once more—lover. His hands, still stuffed in their paws, alternated between gentle brushings and firmer pets along Glade's legs, showing his adoration as he worshipped the best way he knew how.

He read his partner's body as best he could, finding all the spots that led to the reactions he craved. He would focus there, then drift his attention elsewhere, not letting any one spot get played out. Despite the years intervening, he still felt as though he knew Glade's body thoroughly.

"H-huff," Glade breathed with a stiff shudder. "Mmn, such a good little pet."

Michael relaxed back onto his heels, peering up along Glade's more masculine body, eager to receive the praise.

"You did well, roo," Glade growled, hefting himself up further onto the bed. "Come up here by me, there's one more thing I want you to do, and I know you deserve it."

Michael nodded shyly and stood to his feet, feeling the blood flow freely through his cramped legs. He moved around to the side of the bed before climbing in, stretching out alongside his ex.

Glade leaned in closer and bit gently at the lobe of his ear, whispering quietly while he was there, "I want you to paw, just one more time for me. I want to see you get off."

Michael blushed and nodded, still shivering at the bite to his ear. "Yes...yes, Dom Glade."

He moved to slip one of his hands out of the paw mitts, only to feel the sharp crack of the crop against his thigh.

"But leave those on."

Michael swallowed. He knew he'd make a mess of the paws, that was inevitable. He also knew how to clean them, though, and so after a moment, he nodded and rolled onto his back.

His erection hadn't let up since Glade had first gotten his attention with the questions on the dance floor, and by now, he felt an aching need for release. The fur of the paws was dry and coarse against his stiff shaft, and though he usually required lube for masturbation, it seemed to feel just right to curl the clumsy fingers loosely around his cock and stroke along it gently.

It didn't take much, really. The tickling of the fur and the occasional squeeze around the base of his cock as he stroked was enough to get him closer and closer to his orgasm. What finally did it, though, was that last bit of mental stimulation when Glade leaned in close against him and nuzzled up to his ear, murmuring, "You are just such. A good. Boy."

His heavy breaths were cut short with a quiet whimper and he gripped tightly around the base of his shaft with his fur-covered hand and felt the rush of pleasure wash over him, felt the first few spurts of seed land on his front, and the rest dribble down over the brown fur of his paw.

"God, I missed that," Glade cooed as Michael settled back down onto the bed.

"Nnnf."

Glade grinned and gave a gentle kiss to Michael's cheek before levering himself up out of bed. "Thank you, little pet. Now, if you'll excuse me, I've got some other parties to go to."

"Huh? But..." Michael began.

"Hush, you did good."

Michael leaned up onto one elbow, watching Glade tug his boxers and pants back on, then hunt for his shirt. "What...what was that? For us, I mean."

Glade tugged his t-shirt back over his head and stood, regarding Michael for a moment. "Closure," he said simply.

"And where do we go from here?"

"I don't know, roo, I really don't. I just feel like we're in a better place from where we left off before."

Michael nodded.

His head still spun.

⋆

There was an electric-mechanical click as the lock on the door activated, and Michael jolted upright in bed, rushing to cover himself with his hands as he sat up. He must've drifted off once Glade had slipped out of the room to head to his party. He was still wearing the paws, even.

Bomber slipped quietly into the room, saw Michael in his messy and furry state, and smiled bashfully, turning away to face the wall. "Need a moment?"

Michael shook the paws off of his hands quickly and ducked over the edge of the bed to snag his underwear, slipping them on quickly, "Just...ah, just woke up. You're fine."

Bomber laughed and slid further into the room, slipping out of his canvas jacket and sitting down on the bed. "Hope I didnt interrupt, thought you were just sleeping."

"I probably was, at that," Michael mumbled, rubbing his hands over his face, before reaching for his shirt to wipe up his spilled cum.

The two sat in awkward silence for a minute or so before Bomber asked, "Good evening, then?"

Michael let out a breath, more forcefully than he had intended. "Yeah. Glade came over. Bit of...bit of the old days, I guess."

Bomber nodded and fiddled with one of his fingernails.

"Sorry," Michael offered. "Maybe a bit much information."

"It's okay," Bomber responded. "Just wondering what he means to you."

Sensing the undercurrent of meaning, Michael reached a hand over to rest on Bomber's knee. "We broke up, a long time ago. I don't think that's going to change." He took a deep breath before continuing, "I know you like me, Bomber, and I know I've been distant, but I just don't really know where my head is anymore. Glade meant enough to me that I don't know what to do after that ended."

"I can't really say I know how you feel," the mouse replied hesitantly. "I've never been in a situation like that. I don't want to push you or anything, I just like you, I guess."

Michael nodded, silent.

The two sat for a while longer, touching and keeping contact.

Finally, Bomber asked, "Think you guys will hook up again?"

Michael thought for a moment, then shrugged, "Probably not. Not in the same way we did before, certainly, but it's good to have contact open again."

Bomber looked down and nodded.

Michael laughed and leaned over to hug both arms around his friend, “Hey, don’t worry, whatever happens happens, not leaving my friends behind at all.”

Madison Scott-Clary is a transgender writer, editor, and software engineer. She focuses on furry fiction and non-fiction, using that as a framework for exploring across genres. She has edited and written for [adjective][species] since 2011, and edited *Arcana: A Tarot Anthology* for Thurston Howl Publications in 2017. She is the editor-in-chief of Hybrid Ink, LLC, a small publisher focused on thoughtful fiction, exploratory poetry, and creative non-fiction. She lives in the Pacific Northwest with her cat and two dogs, as well as her husband, who is also a dog.

www.makyo.ink
www.hybrid.ink